When I gave the right answer, Ann turned and shot a look at me that was pure poison. She obviously didn't like being shown up, but I just shrugged.

I didn't think anything about it until the next period, which was physical education. In the locker room, the other girls changed into dark blue blouses and balloon-like pants called bloomers.

As we were changing, Ann glanced at me. "You're a little dark, aren't you?"

I blinked, looking down at the back of my hand, and suddenly realized that she wasn't referring to my tan but to my skin color. "You're a little pale, aren't you?" I shot back.

Ann jumped to her feet. "Miss Armstrong better burn that suit after you use it."

I balled my hands into fists. . . .

"Based on experiences from Laurence Yep's own family history, the story offers unique insight into the plight of ethnic minorities. It is disturbing but never depressing, poignant but never melancholy. . . . A pleasure to read, entertaining its audience even as it educates their hearts."   —*The Horn Book*

"[A] moving story . . . Yep skillfully avoids pat explanations."   —*Publishers Weekly*

The Star Fisher

BY LAURENCE YEP

PUFFIN BOOKS

PUFFIN BOOKS

Published by the Penguin Group

Penguin Books USA Inc., 375 Hudson Street, New York, New York 10014, U.S.A.

Penguin Books Ltd, 27 Wrights Lane, London W8 5TZ, England

Penguin Books Australia Ltd, Ringwood, Victoria, Australia

Penguin Books Canada Ltd, 10 Alcorn Avenue, Toronto, Ontario, Canada M4V 3B2

Penguin Books (N.Z.) Ltd, 182–190 Wairau Road, Auckland 10, New Zealand

Penguin Books Ltd, Registered Offices: Harmondsworth, Middlesex, England

First published in the United States of America by William Morrow and Company, Inc., 1991
Reprinted by arrangement with William Morrow and Company, Inc.
Published in Puffin Books, 1992

9   10   8

Library of Congress Cataloging-in-Publication Data
Yep, Laurence.
The star fisher / by Laurence Yep.   p.   cm.
Summary: Fifteen-year-old Joan Lee and her family find the
adjustment hard when they move from Ohio to West Virginia in the 1920's.
ISBN 0-14-036003-4
[1. Chinese Americans—Fiction.   2. Moving, Household—Fiction.
3. Prejudices—Fiction.]   I. Title.
PZ7.Y44St   1992   [Fic]—dc20   92-9234

Printed in the United States of America
Set in ITC Garamond Book

To Sister Rosemary Winklejohann

───Author's Preface───

West Virginia has always been more real to me than China. That's because my grandmother, mother, aunts, and uncle spoke more often of West Virginia than of China. My grandmother's life really began once she reached America at the age of sixteen. If stories about San Francisco's Chinatown might seem alien if heard in West Virginia, tales about West Virginia seem equally exotic when told in San Francisco's Chinatown. For sentimental reasons some twenty years ago, I started to keep a file of their escapades and added to it at every opportunity until I wanted to see West Virginia myself.

It was Sister Rosemary Winklejohann who made the entire West Virginia trip possible. Then, once I had undertaken my pilgrimage to Clarksburg, she asked me if I had thought of writing a novel about my family. It was at that point

I realized I had more than enough in the file to do just that; and after obtaining my mother's permission, I did.

My grandfather really did have a laundry in a converted school in Clarksburg, West Virginia, and my grandmother learned to bake apple pies (and also, I'm told, mouth-watering doughnuts) and once bragged to me that her pies fetched the highest prices at the church socials. There was also a generous-hearted woman, Marie Alcinda Davisson, who is the prototype for Miss Lucy Bradshaw and who told a similar story of her adventures as a girl during the Civil War to my Auntie Mary. A member of one of the oldest families in the region, Miss Alcinda helped welcome one of the newest immigrant families.

However, I have also altered those family stories so that they could be blended together. For instance, it was my Auntie Mary who, at the age of two, used to climb out of her crib and over the backyard fence to have tea with a neighbor. Obviously, I have changed circumstances as well as dates and ages for the sake of the story; and at a certain point the characters themselves grew and developed their own independent personalities, so that I gave up any pretense of using real names.

I should also say that my own family's trek was not unique. Though their numbers were small before the changes in the immigration laws in the 1960s, Chinese families refused to be confined to the Chinatowns on the two coasts and were searching for a place in America for themselves back in the 1920s and earlier. I have met Chinese-Americans who were born and raised in rural towns in such states as Arkansas, Mississippi, and Oklahoma. In this sense, *The Star Fisher* is as much their story as it is my family's.

As in *Dragonwings*, conversations in Chinese are in plain type. Conversations in English are set in italics.

— Spring 1927 —

One

I thought I knew what green was until we went to West Virginia.

As the old locomotive chugged over the pass, I could see nothing but green. Tall, thin trees covered the slopes, and leafy vines grew around the tree trunks; and surrounding the trees were squat bushes and tall grass.

And as the train rattled down into the valley, the green slopes seemed to rise upward like the waves of an ocean; and I felt as if the train were a ship sinking into a sea of green.

As the old day coach swayed back and forth, the other passengers ignored the scenery, concentrating instead on their newspapers or their conversation. One woman was weaving lace, her hands darting with sure, swift motions, so that the white lace seemed to fall magically from her fingertips.

My little brother, Bobby, was thumping his heels rhythmically against the seat. At ten, he was easily bored. During the day, he was like lightning, always having to dart here and there. He would never walk when he could run. And then in the evenings, he would just conk out suddenly. Mama used to wish we could bottle some of his energy and sell it for tonic.

"When are we going to get there?" Bobby asked for the twentieth time.

Bobby had meant his question for me, so he had used English; but Mama spoke to him in Chinese. "Speak in your own language." Though both Mama and Papa wore American clothes, that was about the only thing American about them, since they spoke little English.

"He wanted to know when we would be arriving in town," I translated for Mama, the way I usually did.

However, Mama was staring straight at Bobby. "Let him answer for himself."

Bobby dragged a finger back and forth along the windowsill. "Mama, people stare when we use Chinese."

"Let them stare," Mama said. "I don't want you to forget your Chinese."

"As if I could," Bobby muttered in English.

Papa lowered his month-old *Young China News*. The Chinese newspaper from San Francisco was folded and creased and smudged from having been passed through many hands, but Papa was eager to get the news even if it was a bit stale.

"Answer Mama," he said in Chinese. He tried to look stern, but Papa's mouth was just meant for smiling and not for frowning.

Bobby studied his dirty fingertip. "I just wanted to know when we were going to get there."

"Soon," Papa said and tried to go back to his newspaper.

"Don't slouch." Mama used Bobby's shirt collar to pull him up straight and eyed me. "You're sixteen, Joan. Don't sit as if you were made of jelly."

4

"I'm fifteen, Mama," I corrected her for the dozenth time.

"Americans don't know how to count years," Mama observed calmly. "They should count the year in the womb just like the Chinese."

"Mama," I said, blushing.

My little sister, Emily, was eight going on eighty and had a face made for scowling. She pulled herself reluctantly into an erect posture. "Why did we have to leave Ohio anyway?"

Papa always had more patience with Emily than with the rest of us, Mama included. He folded up his newspaper carefully as if it were made of silk. Then he shifted over beside Emily and set his ear against the window. He kept his ear there for a moment, and then his eyes opened wide in wonder. "Listen," he said to Emily. "Can you hear all the dirty shirts?"

Emily gazed up at Papa suspiciously; and then, slipping off the seat, she set her ear against the glass with that strange air of gravity she always had. The rest of us sat, ears straining as well; but all we could hear was the clickety-clack of the train wheels.

"No," Emily confessed.

Papa scrunched up his face as if the voices were growing louder. "I can hear them whispering. They're so desperate."

That was the thing with Papa, you never knew when he was serious or not; and for want of something better to do, Bobby also squirmed off his seat and joined Emily. "What do they say?"

Papa leaned forward and whispered loudly, "Wash me, wash me."

Mama pulled Bobby back down beside her and shoved Emily back to our seat. "There had better be dirty shirts," Mama declared. "The move has taken most of our money."

Papa didn't say anything. In fact, he didn't even dare look at Mama; and he seemed glad when the conductor waddled through the aisle.

5

"Clarksburg!" he called. *"The next station stop is Clarksburg."*

The lacemaker put away her things and, taking out a hat like a huge plate, began to fasten it to her hairdo with a pin as long as her arm.

Papa seemed glad of the distraction as he got up and began to take our things from the luggage rack overhead. Papa had already brought down the furniture and the heavy laundry equipment, so all we had were our personal belongings.

When I saw what Papa was doing, I got up as well to give him a hand. I stood with my feet slightly spread to keep my balance as I began to convey the things to the aisle. "I'm glad we left," I said, trying to help out Papa. "Ohio was full of ugly factories and smoke."

"Ohio," Emily said, scowling from her seat, "was full of places that showed moving pictures." Emily had especially taken to the new moving pictures and stated often and loudly that she was going to be a cowgirl someday.

"Our old laundry was tiny, but our new laundry will be big. There's more room for business and more room for us." Papa always liked to see the sunny side of things.

Mama was checking around and under the benches to make sure that we hadn't left anything. "But there aren't any other Chinese," Mama complained. She always liked to see the shady side of things.

Huffing and puffing, the train eased into the tan stone station. Setting aside the larger suitcases for himself and Mama, Papa motioned for me to take the next largest suitcase. "They'll come. If you have one successful laundry, other Chinese will want to copy us."

With one hand on the back of the bench for balance, Mama rose unsteadily. "Then they'll cut into our business." She adjusted my posture with her hand. "Now stand up straight. Don't slouch like some loafer."

6

Papa had a penchant for parades. He not only liked to organize them but liked to march in them, so he set us up in a line with a basket for Bobby and an even smaller carpetbag for Emily to carry. "Any strength is a weakness," Papa observed grandly. "And any weakness is also a strength."

"You and your philosophy books." Mama sniffed.

We made our way along the aisle and down the railroad car steps onto the wooden platform. A few other people had gotten off in Clarksburg, among them the lacemaker, with a small valise.

On an old wooden bench in front of the station lounged a man with red hair. He was wearing old coveralls, but the bib barely contained his huge stomach. Taking a can from a pocket, he took out a pinch of snuff with all the regal majesty of a king and stuck it under his tongue.

"Darn monkeys," he said, staring at us.

Mama turned to me sharply. "What did he say?" she asked.

Papa spoke even less English than Mama, but he could read the man's expression. "Never mind. Just ignore him. That kind doesn't even have a spare shirt to wash."

As we began to walk along the platform, I glanced behind me, looking over Bobby's head at Emily. "That's right," I said meaningfully. "We don't want any trouble."

Emily gazed at me, the picture of innocence. "Bobby wouldn't think of it," she said sweetly.

In the meantime, though, Mister Snuff had begun to swear; and the more he swore, the louder he got — like a dog working up its nerve to bite someone.

As they neared the man, Mama and Papa both kept their eyes straight ahead. I tried to copy their example, but it was hard because passing by him was like trying to walk near the edge of a volcanic crater. I knew, though, that Bobby would do the same; but I wasn't sure about Emily. Too late, I regretted that I hadn't followed her.

7

Mama and Papa had just started down the platform steps to the street when I heard Mister Snuff shout in pain. Whirling around, I saw Emily with her heel on his foot. We all wore big, ugly shoes that were as heavy as rocks—the kind that mothers called sensible. As Emily had passed, she had stepped on Mister Snuff's foot, on purpose.

"Unh?" Emily asked innocently.

"Why, you little monkey, I'll teach you to watch where you're going." Mister Snuff swung up a hand that looked as big as a shovel.

I dropped the suitcase on the platform and darted in between Emily and the man. *"Sorry, mister. Sorry."* I smiled at him apologetically. *"My sister's a little simple."* I added with a glance at Emily, *"Even stupid."*

Mister Snuff lowered his hand slowly. *"She talks American."*

"Of course we do," Emily snapped. *"We were born here. We go to American schools."*

Mister Snuff's jaw dropped open. *"They both talk."*

Turning, I could see Emily's mouth twisting open for some angry retort. Quickly I clapped my hand over her mouth. *"Don't drool, dear,"* I said and kept my hand over her mouth.

"Quit it," Emily mumbled and tried to step back, but I stayed stuck to her like glue.

Still with my hand over her mouth, I leaned over to whisper fiercely in her ear, "Say another word, and I'll pinch you so hard you won't ever sit down again." And I began to back along the platform, dragging Emily with me.

Somehow Bobby had picked up my suitcase along with his own basket. He staggered after us as I rushed Emily toward the platform steps.

"Wait," my little sister kept mumbling in both Chinese and English, *"wait."* But I wouldn't give her a chance. Instead, I spun her around and practically carried her and her carpetbag down the steps and onto the street.

On the sidewalk, Mama and Papa had just noticed that we were missing. Looking over her shoulder at us, Mama scolded, "Don't wander. This is a strange city."

"You don't know how strange," Emily grunted and began to swing her feet in the air. "Put me down, Joan."

Papa came back toward us with his hand held out. "She's just an itty-bitty thing for that big old bag."

Emily made a face at me as she handed the bag to Papa. And I'm afraid I made a face back as I retrieved my suitcase from Bobby.

We walked along the sidewalk past small, boxlike houses. There were white picket fences and little patches of vegetables. Flowers grew in window boxes, glowing with bright colors in the warm afternoon sun. Compared to the industrial town we had left in Ohio, everything looked as neat and cozy as a toy town built out of blocks.

"Each house has clotheslines," Mama said to Papa.

Papa gave a laugh. "Certainly they can wash. But"—he arched his eyebrows up and down at Mama—"can they iron? And"—he paused dramatically—"can they starch?"

At the corner of a block, Papa stopped beside a white-washed fence that rose only as high as his waist. Beyond the gate was a brick building with white columns on either side of the big doorway. Old maple trees grew like sentinels almost up to the rooftop on the second floor.

"Is that it?" I asked, awestruck.

"No, no, that belongs to our landlady, Miss Lucy." Papa led us down the cross street to a smaller, white building.

"This is it," Papa announced.

Bobby craned his head back as he ogled the building. "This is still pretty big."

But Emily halted dead in her tracks and gawked at the sign. Then she spun on a heel and glared accusingly at Papa. "It says _School_."

"It was a private school run by Miss Lucy. But when she retired, she closed it down, so she was glad to rent this big

9

old place to us." Setting down the bags, Papa fished a key out of his pocket. "It's got all the space we need for washing the whole state of West Virginia. You open the door, my little squash." He held the key out toward Emily in a conciliatory gesture.

Emily, though, stayed right where she was. "I don't want to live in any school."

Papa dangled the key between his fingers. "It's not a school anymore. It's our laundry."

However, Emily could be as self-conscious as Bobby. Beyond that, I think the incident with the man at the station had made her dislike this place even more than before, so she was glad to find some excuse for leaving. "It's like living in jail."

Mama set her suitcase down smartly. "People," she declared, "not a building, make a home." Taking the key from Papa's fingers, she opened the gate, marched up the steps, and put the key in the lock. It stuck for a moment, and Mama struggled with the key. Suddenly her forehead creased in worry. "I hope this isn't a sign." Of all of us, Mama could be very superstitious.

Papa followed her up the steps and stood beside her. "The only thing that it's a sign of is that the lock is rusty." He wrapped his long, elegant fingers around her wrist — fingers that were better suited to painting and calligraphy than to being thrust into boiling-hot water.

With Papa's help, Mama managed to turn the key in the lock so that the door swung open with a loud creak. There was a dim hallway that seemed to stretch on forever with rooms on either side.

With a dreamy smile, Papa began to point. "We'll have the counter in front, and back there along that wall we'll have the shelves for the parcels." He indicated another room. "We'll use the next room for drying and the room beyond that for washing."

10

I staggered through the gate. "Where will we sleep?"

"Upstairs." Papa motioned for us to come inside with great sweeping motions of his arms. "You and Emily have a classroom as big as the train depot, and Bobby has a room that used to be an office."

Bobby walked on past Emily, the basket banging against his legs. "Are you coming?"

Emily folded her arms resolutely around her stomach. "Nope."

"Show Bobby his room," Mama said.

"I'll take care of things here." With a sigh, I set my suitcase inside the doorway. "You go up with Papa," I said to Mama.

We could already hear Bobby's happy shouts floating down the stairway. Mama started inside but stopped. "We'll leave a pillow and a blanket out here," she said to Emily.

I finished transferring the bags into the safety of the hallway. Papa had already gotten out his hammer and nails and was beginning to knock a counter together from scraps of wood. All the while, Emily had stood in the middle of the sidewalk, glowering like a miniature gargoyle. For once she seemed determined to be more stubborn than Mama.

I didn't want to leave her alone in a strange town, so I took a book from my coat pocket. Then, taking off my coat, I set it down on a step as a cushion.

Emily stood curiously on tiptoe as if that could help her see the book. *"What book is that?"*

I held up the cover up for her to see. "Frank Merriwell. *It was a gift from Agnes."* Agnes is—or rather was—my best friend in Ohio.

"Read to me," Emily ordered imperiously.

"When I have to read out loud, it takes too long." I patted the step beside me. *"But you can read over my shoulder,"* I coaxed. *"I'll even wait for you to finish before I turn the pages."*

11

But I couldn't lure Emily in even that far. *"Nope."*

"Suit yourself, misery," I said and began to read despite Papa's hammering, but I kept one eye on Emily.

As people passed in the street, they stared at us but did not say anything. More and more, I began to feel as if that man on the platform had been right: in this town, we were like monkeys in a zoo. And out on the sidewalk, Emily began to look small and scared as if she felt like the only other monkey in the zoo.

Two

When I saw the woman, she reminded me of a bird. Though her hair was white with age, she walked with small, quick, lively steps. She was dressed in a long skirt that reached to the sidewalk almost, and she wore a little jacket with a kind of cape that was fastened in front with a large cameo brooch. There was a huge hat pinned to her head as well, and she carried a big basket over one arm.

When she saw us, she cocked her head to one side and leaned forward, the feather in her hat nodding. Her free hand tilted up the pair of wire glasses perched on her nose as she looked us up and down. *"Hello. Are you my new neighbors?"*

She sounded as if she were talking to someone her own age. Emily glanced around, but at the moment we were the only ones on the street

The woman pursed her lips for a moment and then tried again. *"Do you speak English?"* Her eyes were bright with curiosity.

Putting away my novel, I got up. *"Yes, ma'am."*

She smiled at me and then put her hand under Emily's chin and studied her face. *"Goodness. What a cookie face."*

Emily stared up at her in fascination. *"Cookie face?"*

She studied Emily with the grave face of a doctor by a dying patient. *"What that face needs is a cookie. Then you'll start smiling."* Pinned by a chain to her jacket was a little watch with a gold knob at the top and a porcelain back with soft pink roses painted on it. When she straightened up, she glanced at the watch. *"It's almost four. Won't you come and have some tea?"*

I suddenly realized how thirsty I was; and from the way Emily was licking her lips, I knew she was, too. But before she could speak up, I did. *"Thank you, but I don't think we can."*

The woman's free hand darted to the handle of the basket so she could hold it in front of her. *"What intelligent children. Of course you shouldn't if you don't know me. I'm Miss Lucy Bradshaw, your landlady, and I live right next to you."* She nodded to a red brick building next to the school. *"And you're . . . ?"*

"Joan," I said with a self-conscious nod.

"And I'm Emily," she chimed in.

"Well, Emily, why don't you ask your parents if you can come to tea?" When Miss Lucy smiled, it made her long nose look even more like a beak. *"I'll wait here."*

Though we had been in the houses of our friends before, we had never sat down to tea. I knew enough from novels that tea was an important occasion for Americans. I had read descriptions of teas, of course, but I had never been at one; and that's a little like reading descriptions of an elephant and trying to match those with a real live one. Sheer curiosity made me want to go to her tea.

14

I felt Emily tugging at my skirt, and when I leaned over, she warned in a whisper, "Once we're inside the laundry, we probably won't ever get out again."

"I'll talk to Papa," I answered back. Papa was always the one we went to when we needed something. I figured that it was all right to leave Emily alone with Miss Lucy for a few minutes. Opening the gate, I skipped up the steps and opened the door.

Mama was right there, industriously rubbing at some imaginary spot on the wainscoting. But I was sure she had been waiting by the door to make certain that we were all right.

"I'll help you in a little bit, Mama," I promised. "May we go to tea with the landlady?"

"Yes, you may," Mama grunted as she went on with her rubbing. But as I turned to the front door again, she added, "And don't go running to your papa every time you want something. I understand that much English."

Emily was leaning against the fence and chatting away with Miss Lucy when I came outside. *"Mama said it was all right,"* I announced as I closed the door.

Emily stared at me in amazement, but I ignored her as I opened the gate and stepped onto the street. *"This way,"* Miss Lucy said and led us along the sidewalk around the corner. The front door to her house faced Main, while the school faced Second.

Miss Lucy nodded down to Emily. *"After you, Emily."* Wiping her feet on the welcome mat, she opened the door *"Come in,"* she said brightly.

Emily would have dashed in, but I caught her and made her drag her feet over the mat before I did.

There was a funny smell to the house—not unpleasant, but odd. And it took me a moment to realize it smelled like the museum we'd been to in Toledo. Miss Lucy had set her basket down and was unpinning her hat.

In the parlor, an upright piano squatted like a silent bull

15

while thick, red velvet drapes fought back the sun. Overhead, a chandelier hung from the ceiling like a crystal spider. Beneath it, on a reading stand, sat an old Bible, its black leather cover much worn and the gold embossing almost rubbed away. Through the gold-edged sides of the paper stuck a little red ribbon like a snake's tongue.

"What's that?" Emily asked. She backed up so fast she bumped into me.

Miss Lucy set her hat down on a small table against the wall. *"That's Rusty."*

The dog sat on its haunches under a glass dome on the broad table. Its red hair and big floppy ears did not move as Emily and I peered so close that our breath began to frost the glass.

Coming over, Miss Lucy crooked an index finger and tapped the glass with it. Instantly Emily hopped back against me as if she expected the dog to bark. *"Rusty's dead,"* Miss Lucy explained. *"My grandfather's hobby was stuffing animals, and Rusty was my grandfather's favorite hunting dog."* She waved her hand at the floor above us. *"The rest of the animals are upstairs."*

I couldn't help staring past the chandelier toward the white ceiling. Patterns of fruit and vegetables decorated it as well. I could almost imagine all the dark, furry shapes lurking up there. *"What sort of animals?"*

"Well, let's see. There's another dog and three cats." Miss Lucy looked up at the ceiling, too, as if she could see right through it. *"A possum, an owl."* She began to tick off the menagerie on her fingers. *"A woodpecker, a raccoon that got in the way of Grandfather's buggy, and more birds than you could shake a stick at. In fact, there wasn't a dead pet that was safe from Grandfather."*

"No lions or tigers?" Emily wondered, remembering the museum in Toledo.

Miss Lucy patted her hair, which had been done up in a bun. *"There was a bear that Grandfather wanted to stuff. But*

16

Grandmother had enough of his dust catchers, so she put her foot down." She gave a little giggle that made her seem fifty years younger. "_He got so mad that he threatened to stuff her if she died first._"

I couldn't tell if she was joking or not, but Emily frowned up at Miss Lucy solemnly. "_Did she?_"

"_No, he did._" Miss Lucy took a handkerchief from her sleeve to wipe at the glass. "_But his threat gave Grandmother quite a scare. I think they each stayed alive an extra ten years out of sheer stubbornness._"

Emily suddenly darted over toward a huge cabinet that rose almost to the ceiling. On shelf after shelf were rows of eggs of all sizes and colors. "_Did you dye these eggs?_"

Miss Lucy treated Emily as if they were the same age. "_No,_" she said as she came over, "_my great-aunt liked to collect them. She could shinny up a tree faster than a squirrel — and that was in full skirts._"

Emily pressed her nose so close to the glass that I pulled her back. Before every egg was a card with curly, delicate writing. "_Robin redbreast,_" she read slowly.

Miss Lucy clasped her hands in front of her. "_She said there was never a blue as nice as a robin's egg._"

I studied the egg with Emily. "_It's bluer than the sky._"

Miss Lucy looked at me thoughtfully. "_Why, I guess it is._"

I found myself liking Miss Lucy more and more. She wasn't stuck up like other grown-ups. Instead, she talked and acted toward us as if we were all equals.

Emily slipped away from my grasp and turned in a slow circle. Wherever she looked, there were cabinets full of odd objects. "_You certainly have a lot of things._"

"_Every member of my family had a hobby._" Miss Lucy spread out her arms grandly. "_This house is full of hobbies._" She lowered her arms and added, "_And memories._"

For a moment, surrounded by all of her family's memories in that great big house, Miss Lucy looked as small as Emily. As a giant grandfather clock loudly ticked off the seconds, Miss Lucy reminded me of a little girl lost in a museum.

Suddenly I felt sorry for her. I knew she must feel lonely—maybe as lonely as I had felt in the street. *"What's your hobby?"*

Miss Lucy unpinned her brooch and hung her cape over the back of a chair. *"People are my hobby. What's yours?"*

Emily piped up before I could. *"Food is my hobby."*

"Then"—Miss Lucy winked mischievously—*"it's a good thing I invited you to tea."*

I felt more and more as if we three were playing house, and Miss Lucy was only pretending to be our host and we were only pretending to be her guests. And suddenly I didn't feel strange or different. *"Yes, it's so very kind of you."* I dropped a curtsy as I had seen in a moving picture, and Emily did the same.

And to give Miss Lucy credit, she started to play the game as well. She might have had white hair, but she could be as lively as a little girl. *"This way."* Plucking up her dress between her fingers, she picked up her basket and led us grandly past more dim rooms full of furniture and brought us into the kitchen.

It was the sunniest room in her house and more typical of her than any other of those gloomy rooms. Thin lace curtains did not keep out the light but made shadowy patterns on the walls, and the back door was cut in half. That way the bottom half could be kept locked while Miss Lucy kept the top half open for air and light. Unbolting the top half, she swung it back, revealing a small dirt courtyard between her house and our laundry. In one corner was a neat little garden of vegetables. Each row had a stake with a piece of paper that said what was in the row. I couldn't help thinking to myself that she had been a schoolteacher all right.

In the center of the kitchen was a big table with a worn top, and on pegs on its sides were rolling pins and other baking instruments hanging by leather thongs. Emily dragged out a chair and promptly sat down.

Unbuttoning her jacket, Miss Lucy hung that from a peg on the wall and took down an apron from another peg. _"But if people weren't my hobby, then food would be it."_

I helped her tie the apron behind her. _"Can I help?"_

There was a gas stove against one wall, looking as big and unmovable as a mountain. Next to the oven was a smaller door for the wood, and above the stove was a compartment for keeping things warm. Miss Lucy went over to it now and took a big teakettle from the top. _"Yes, you can get out plates, cups, and saucers."_ And she nodded her head toward a cabinet against the far wall.

As I passed by the table, I poked Emily. "Ask her if she needs any help," I said, ignoring the glare she shot at me.

"I want to help, too," Emily announced.

"You can set the places," Miss Lucy said.

Emily scratched her head doubtfully, but she was afraid to ask what Miss Lucy meant. When she looked at me, I could only shake my head that I didn't know either. But I was just as reluctant to request an explanation as Emily. Even though we had been born here and could name all the presidents and the capitals of the states, there were so many little things that we didn't know—like place settings. In some ways, we were often like actors who were thrust onstage without a script, so that we had to improvise. And too often, up in Ohio, our ignorance had gotten us laughed at; and no one likes to feel like a fool.

But Miss Lucy must have been the kind of schoolteacher who had enormous reservoirs of patience. _"A place setting,"_ she said. _"You know, knives and forks and napkins."_

"Oh, yes, of course." Emily nodded her head wisely like a little owl. _"That kind of place setting."_

With a sigh of relief that that crisis had passed, I went to the cabinet; but all I could find were cups and plates of thin, delicate china on which birds were painted. They were too fine for everyday use, so I turned to Miss Lucy. _"Am I by the right cabinet?"_

Going over to the sink, Miss Lucy turned the tap and water splashed into the metal kettle with a hollow drumming sound. *"Yes, that's it."*

With Miss Lucy to direct her, Emily had found the napkins and put them out. Since she was not sure how many utensils to use, she was setting out three spoons, two knives, and four forks at each place. Taking one of the plates, I held it up uncertainly. *"One of these?"*

Miss Lucy had set the kettle on the stove. *"You're company, aren't you?"* Miss Lucy looked at us over her shoulder. *"I need a plate, Emily."*

Emily came running over and took the plate when I handed it to her. When she brought it back, Miss Lucy had opened up a cookie tin and began to heap the plate with all sorts of different cookies, which she set on the table. *"Have some?"*

I was hungry enough to eat the whole plate, but I was also determined that Emily and I were going to behave like grown-up guests. "Don't be a pig," I said to Emily.

Glumly, Emily took the plate to the table and set it down in the center. *"I'll wait, ma'am."*

I set out cups of paper-thin china on saucers and put plates down by each setting. When the water had boiled, Miss Lucy poured it into a pot and added some tea leaves. When she had brought the teapot to the table and sat down, Emily, who had not taken her eyes from the plate, asked in Chinese, "Now can I eat?"

However, I knew Emily's habits all too well. "Just one," I instructed her in Chinese.

Emily looked at me in outrage. "One?"

"One," I said with a firm nod.

Emily leaned this way and that while she examined the contents of the plate for the largest cookie. Then, with all the delicacy of a surgeon, she slipped her choice out from the bottom and placed it in triumph upon her plate.

Miss Lucy must have guessed some of what we had said in Chinese. _"Well, I have an appetite, so excuse me."_ She put a half-dozen cookies on top of her own plate. Then she tilted up the teapot so that a little bit of red-brown liquid poured from the pot into her cup. Deciding that it was all right, she finished filling the cup, the tea tinkling musically on the thin sides. _"Tea?"_ she asked Emily.

Emily looked dubiously at the cup because the tea looked much darker and stronger than the tea we usually drank. _"I guess so."_

Picking up the saucer with the cup, Miss Lucy placed it in front of Emily and took Emily's in turn. _"Tea?"_ she asked me.

"Please." I spread my napkin across my lap.

When she had poured my cup and handed it to me, she took mine and poured one for herself. In the meantime, Emily had been sniffing her tea suspiciously.

"Don't do that," I warned. "It's not polite."

"It smells funny," Emily protested.

Miss Lucy had been waiting politely for us to finish. Now she held up a small silver bowl shaped like a pumpkin. _"Sugar?"_

I had never before heard of having sugar in tea. In fact, we always drank ours plain; but neither Emily nor I wanted to behave like children.

"Please," Emily said politely.

Miss Lucy picked up a small spoon. _"One spoonful or two?"_

It was another anxious moment. _"Unh . . ."_ Emily guessed wildly, _"six."_

"My, you have quite a sweet tooth." Miss Lucy did not even blink an eye as she spooned the sugar into Emily's cup. And then she turned to me. _"And you, Joan?"_

Six sounded like a nice, round, grown-up number to me, too. _"I'll have six."_

"I can see that sweet tooth runs in the family." But she

21

added the sugar to the little cup as well until the cup was more sugar than tea.

I thought I should make polite conversation. *"My father says that when you do something, do it well."*

"He's a wise man." She held up a small silvery pitcher. *"Milk?"*

We'd never had milk in our tea either, but Emily gamely said, *"Please."*

"Say when," Miss Lucy instructed her and began pouring.

She might still be pouring if she had waited for Emily to tell her to stop. As it was, she stopped when she filled the cup to the brim. Taking my lesson from Emily, I told her to stop when my cup was almost full.

Emily and I were old hands at watching a host. When Miss Lucy put only one spoonful of sugar and a dash of milk into her tea, we both realized our mistakes. And when she stirred her cup, we tried to imitate her; but stirring was a bit harder for us at first with all the sugar inside the cup. Nonetheless, the spoon rang against the sides like the clapper in a delicate bell.

And when she raised the cup, she put out her little finger. With a glance at me, Emily stuck out her pinkie and raised her cup; and I did the same.

The tea was sweet enough to make my teeth shiver, so I put my cup down. Emily, however, had quite the sweet tooth and went on drinking.

Soon we were chatting like three old friends. Miss Lucy asked about our old town in Ohio, and we asked about our new home. (It had been the birthplace of the Confederate general Stonewall Jackson.) She asked about my family, and we asked about hers—she had a great-grandfather who'd fought in the Revolutionary War. Emily and I were both feeling very proud of ourselves when someone knocked on the door.

Immediately Miss Lucy became a grown-up again. *"Excuse me,"* she said. Dabbing her napkin at her lips, she put it on the table and went to the door.

"Yes?" Miss Lucy asked in her friendly way.

"Excuse me. I thought I heard my sisters." It was Bobby. *"My mother sent me here for them."*

"Of course, they're right here." Miss Lucy opened the bottom half of the door and stepped aside so Bobby could see us.

The game was over, but Emily wanted to finish it right. She held up her teacup. *"I'll be with you as soon as I finish my tea."*

"You're coming home now." An exasperated Bobby stormed into the kitchen and grabbed Emily's hand.

Embarrassed that her brother was treating her like a child, Emily got so angry that she forgot her manners and tried to kick him. "Let go."

But Bobby pulled stubbornly. "We can't start dinner until you're home."

"Watch out," I said, getting up from my chair. To my horror, I saw the fragile cup slip out of Emily's hand. It seemed to fall in slow motion: the tea flowing out of the cup, the cup itself tumbling through the air. Bobby tried to catch it, but his hands moved even slower.

It crashed with a tinkling sound. Dozens of pieces sprayed across the floor. "You broke it," Emily wailed.

Bobby had grown very pale, while I knelt down right in the tea and began picking up the pieces. *"We're sorry,"* I said to Miss Lucy. *"We'll do chores until we pay you back."* That would probably take us into next year from the look of that exquisite cup.

"Fiddlesticks." Miss Lucy had gotten a broom. *"I have tons of cups just like that."* She tapped me with the broom straws until I stood up. *"Collecting china was my mother's hobby."*

23

That only made me feel worse, though. *"Then it must have some sentimental value,"* I objected.

"New memories are just as good as old ones. I haven't had such a nice tea in ages." She winked at me as if our game were our special secret. And I knew the little girl was still there inside Miss Lucy. She was just hiding from Bobby and the rest of the world.

I tried to play the grown-up guest. *"Then,"* I said with a polite smile, *"we must have tea again."*

Miss Lucy smiled—she seemed glad of any excuse to smile. She started to open her mouth to answer when her nose began to twitch. Surprised, she rubbed it. *"Goodness. I smell smoke."*

"It is smoke," Emily said and pointed.

Spinning around, I saw smoke pouring from the school-house across the courtyard. "Fire," I shouted and dashed outside.

Three

I burst through Miss Lucy's doorway and out into the court-yard. "Papa, Papa," I shouted.

Flailing her hands at the smoke, Mama stumbled out of the laundry. "Papa's all right," she said and then added, "and so am I."

I caught Mama before she could stumble into Miss Lucy's vegetable patch. "Were you cooking?"

Mama tried to answer, but she began to cough, so she could only nod her head. Bobby and Emily had come running over by then. "Take care of Mama," I ordered them and then turned toward the laundry. Running into smoking houses wasn't my idea of fun, but I wanted to make sure about Papa.

But then he appeared in the rear doorway with a towel

in his hands. "It's crackers and water tonight," he announced and began to wave the towel.

Bobby was busy patting Mama on the back to help her lungs get rid of the smoke. "Again?"

Mama's face had turned tomato red in her embarrassment. "Again," she rasped hoarsely.

Miss Lucy came out of her kitchen with a bucket full of water. Hurrying as best she could with the heavy load, she sloshed water accidentally onto her apron. *"Is it a fire, Mr. Lee?"*

Draping the towel over his shoulder, Papa went over to Mama, who was standing up on her own now. *"No need,"* he said in English; but he always had trouble pronouncing American words.

Miss Lucy staggered across the courtyard under the heavy weight of the bucket. *"Excuse me. What did you say?"*

Signing to Bobby to help Miss Lucy, Papa repeated himself more slowly. *"No need. Everything hunky-dory."*

As Bobby took the bucket from Miss Lucy, she wiped at her damp apron. *"And is this your wife, Mr. Lee?"*

"Yes."

"Mrs. Lee."

Taking Mama's elbow, Papa turned her around. *"And these are my children."* Next he introduced Bobby because he was a boy. Papa could be very traditional sometimes.

It didn't go unnoticed by Miss Lucy; and when he tried to introduce me, Miss Lucy simply smiled. *"We've met already."* She nodded to Emily. *"And also this young lady."*

"Yes?" Papa was a little puzzled, but he waved his hand at the white-haired lady with the wet apron. "This is our landlady," he said in Chinese, "Miss Lucy."

Miss Lucy peered at the kitchen cautiously as a wisp of smoke drifted outward. *"What happened?"*

"I . . ." Mama's tongue struggled to form the words. *"I young. . . ."* However, the explanation was beyond Mama's

few words of English, so she looked over at me for help the way she always did in these situations.

I was used to it by now. _"Mama,"_ I explained, _"was the youngest in her family, so no one bothered to teach her how to cook."_

The vegetable patch caught Miss Lucy's eye. As if she didn't want to waste the water, she took the bucket back from Bobby and began to empty the bucket carefully along its even rows. _"Then you'll just have to come and have dinner with me."_

"Oh, boy," Emily said.

I had to agree with her sentiments. If Miss Lucy's cooking was anything like her cookie baking, we were in for a feast. I was just thinking that some good might have come out of the fire after all, but Papa wagged his hands back and forth.

_"No, no,"_ he said.

"It's the neighborly thing to do," Miss Lucy said. As a ribbon of smoke floated by her face, her eyes followed it. _"And maybe I'll teach Mrs. Lee a few simple things to cook, too."_ Suddenly she clapped a hand over her mouth. _"Oh, my stars, will you listen to me chatter on! Once a teacher, always a teacher."_ She laughed. It was a young laugh, so I knew it came from deep inside her.

Mama seemed encouraged by the merry sound, and she glanced at me. Once I had translated for her, Mama frowned in puzzlement. "Why does she want to do that? We're perfect strangers."

At the same time that Mama had been speaking in Chinese, Miss Lucy was speaking in English. _"I ought to be ashamed of myself. I shouldn't pester people like this."_

When people did that, it sometimes made me feel as dizzy as a spinning top. It took a moment to translate for the both of them. When everything was sorted out, Mama rubbed her chin with her thumb. "What's that woman up to?" she asked me suspiciously. "Is she trying to find out how

27

much we have so she can raise the rent?"

"She's not up to anything, Mama," I said indignantly.

Miss Lucy smiled apologetically. *"I guess I still enjoy teaching."*

I was waiting just in case Miss Lucy had anything else to say, but Mama nudged me in the ribs. "What did she say?"

Sometimes Mama expected me to read her mind as to what she wanted. Annoyed, I rubbed my side as I told Mama what Miss Lucy had said. As soon as I was finished, though, Papa stiffened. *"No."*

Emily pivoted on her heel. *"But, Papa—"* she started to protest.

If anyone could get something from Papa, it was Emily; but Papa shook his head again. *"No."* He looked at Emily, but we knew his words were for all of us. "If anyone will teach my family, it will be me. I'm the teacher." He added bitterly, "Or should have been."

And then we knew that it wasn't any use. Papa didn't make up his mind often, but when he did, it was like trying to stop a locomotive. Still, Mama tried to put the best face on it. "It's so late," she said and elbowed me in annoyance when I waited for more, so I kept on translating while Mama spoke in Chinese, smiling all the while. "And we've had such a long trip. If you don't mind, we'll postpone the lessons."

Miss Lucy seemed disappointed. *"I'll give you a rain check, then."*

I tried to translate Miss Lucy's reply for Mama but stumbled over "rain check." *"I don't know those words,"* I had to confess to Miss Lucy.

Miss Lucy pantomimed slapping her own wrist with a ruler. *"That's what I get for being so slangy. A rain check is what you get when a baseball game is rained on. It may be a receipt or just your ticket stub."*

Bobby looked in awe at Miss Lucy. *"You've been to a baseball game?"* For the longest time in Ohio, he'd been

28

wanting to see the Canton Bulldogs. But paying good money to see grown-up men play games had been beyond both Mama and·Papa.

"I might have been," Miss Lucy said with a cat-that-ate-the-canary smile.

Mama chafed during this short delay and plucked at my sleeve—which was her shorthand way of telling me to get on with it.

Papa, of course, eavesdropped while I gave a brief explanation to Mama; and Miss Lucy seemed to drop even more in his estimation. When we had said our good-byes, we went back inside the laundry. There was a small cookstove, a table, some chairs, and a blackened pot. There were times when Mama couldn't even boil water—though she tried her hardest.

Mama went straight to her American-style purse on the table and carefully counted out some pennies. "I saw a store on the way here. Take your sister," she said to Bobby, "and get some crackers for dinner."

We could hear Bobby's stomach growling, wanting more substantial fare, but he knew better than to argue. "Yes, Mama." But when he tried to take Emily's hand, she pulled away stubbornly. "No, I don't want to go anywhere."

Mama just kept staring into her purse. I knew a storm was brewing and didn't want Emily to see. _"Go with Bobby, Emily."_

And something in my tone must have warned Emily because to my relief she shut up and took Bobby's hand. I found some steel wool and started on the pot.

The front door had no sooner closed than Mama snapped her purse shut. "What's the matter with you?" she asked Papa. "I'm sorry I ruined dinner, but that's no reason the children have to go hungry."

However, Papa, who was usually so mild-mannered, closed the door and swore. "The idea of that woman calling

29

herself a teacher! What does she know? How can you write great poetry, great novels, great thoughts in that gobble-gobble talk of the Americans?"

Mama rounded on Papa. "You're the one who wanted to come to the land of the Golden Mountain." Mama used the fancy name for America.

Papa clenched his fists in frustration. "There was nothing for me at home. Nothing! I waited for years for the Manchus to be gone. And then when they are, they set up a republic. And the republic abolished the scholarship exams in its almighty wisdom."

For almost three centuries, a group of barbarians had held the dragon throne. But sixteen years ago, they had been chased out finally.

Mama refused to be intimidated. "It's a Western-style republic. They want people with Western ideas. Well, you're here now. Learn some of them."

"You're just as bad as the rest of them." Papa flung out a hand angrily. "You'd turn your back on four thousand years of tradition and learning."

"The empire is gone," Mama said. "It's a new age."

For millennia, men had to study the classics and pass exams on them in order to gain a government post. It was thought that men who could best understand the wisdom of the ages could best serve the people.

"Yes," Papa agreed. "It used to be fragrant ink, stinking money." It was a proverb that Papa had once explained. A scholar has ink sticks in which a little scent has been mixed, but a merchant only handles dirty, greasy money. "It's an age where people of talent have to dig ditches." He held up his hands. "I was famous for my calligraphy. Now look at these hands after being in tubs of hot water for years."

Mama looked up at him, eye to eye. "You're a merchant now, not a scholar."

Papa lowered his hands gloomily. "With nothing but

debts to pay." He stormed past Mama abruptly and went out into the hallway. Mama just stood there, staring at the wall. When we heard him rummaging around among the suitcases, Mama called out, "Your books are in the brown suitcase."

"Where did you pack my ink sticks and brushes?" Papa called sullenly.

"They're in the black suitcase with the abacus," Mama said.

"And the other business things?" Papa said angrily.

"Yes," Mama called, though she shouldn't have.

The only response was a door slamming.

"Papa will need water to mix his ink." Mama found an old dusty cup on a shelf and gave it to me. "Wash this out and then bring him some. I'll do the pot."

I began to wash my soot-blackened right hand. "I don't think I can scrape out that last layer of rice. It's like charcoal."

"I'll get it out." Mama took the pot. "I've had a lot of practice. Just make sure you bring the water to Papa. He always feels better when he's written a poem."

I found a rag and wiped my hands off. "Yes, Mama." Mama moved over a little so I could wash out the cup.

Outside we could hear the quick patter of shoes, and Emily came in through the back door with a package under her arm. "Bobby says to go ahead without him."

Mama turned around from the sink. "But he must be hungry."

A loud man's voice rolled into the laundry like an ugly little porcupine. When another man joined him in harsh laughter, Emily pressed her lips together tightly. "Bobby's busy."

"It can wait." Mama went back to scrubbing the pot. "It's our first meal in our new home."

Emily refused to look at either of us. "Bobby has to clean up something."

31

Suddenly, over the ugly laughter outside, we could hear Bobby shouting in Chinese, "You bad, bad men." When he got angry, Bobby sometimes forgot what language he was using.

"Stay here," Mama said to us. She patted the air as if she were placing an invisible wall to shut us in. Whirling around, she began to run down the hallway.

A door opened and we heard Papa ask, "What's going on?"

"I don't know," I said, and Papa chased after Mama.

I looked at Emily and she looked at me, and then we both charged after Mama and Papa.

When we thundered through the front door, we found Mama outside the gate holding Bobby, while Papa wrung the excess moisture from a handkerchief that I recognized as Bobby's. He must have wet it in the rain barrel under the roof gutters. Even as we stepped outside, Papa began to wash furiously at something on the front of the fence.

Mama looked over Bobby's head at Papa. "Paint is the only way to get that off."

Papa gritted his teeth in frustration. "I know."

Mama beckoned me over and then gestured at the fence. "Tell me what this says."

Bobby, however, already knew the words. He clung to Mama. "It says, 'Go home,'" and he added a bad word.

Mama raised both arms protectively like a hen with her chicks. I found myself pressing myself against her along with Emily, while Mama lowered her arms around us and held us tight.

"Want us to read it to you?" came a shout from across the street

Across the street was Mister Snuff from the railroad depot. With him was a man lean as a fence railing. They were both laughing as they lounged against the brick wall of a church. But there was a mean, lazy look to them as if they

32

knew they were bigger and stronger than anyone else on the block.

Still squatting on the sidewalk, Papa whirled around. *"You do this?"*

Mister Snuff stood up straight as he spread out his arms in an elaborate show of innocence. *"Do you see any paint?"*

Emily shoved Mama away angrily. *"Better go back to school, if you ever did. 'Home' is spelled H-O-M-E, not H-O-O-M."*

Mister Snuff straightened. *"You calling me ignorant?"*

"I don't have to," Emily jeered. *"You already are."*

Papa shot to his feet. "Get her inside."

Mama already had her hand over Emily's mouth and was dragging her back toward the laundry. "Get inside," Papa said urgently. The gate banged behind him as he waved the wet handkerchief at us.

Behind us, the two men had begun to swagger away, singing a rude song. We could hear them dimly through the thick door after Papa had closed it. With his back pressed against the door, he looked at us. "What have I gotten us into?"

"You couldn't know," Mama said. In the face of the new threat, their old quarrel was quite forgotten.

"I'm not afraid of them," Emily said defiantly.

"Well, you should be," Papa said. "Chinese have been lynched for less than that." He squatted down before Emily. "Don't forget the old proverb, 'The nail that sticks out gets hammered.'"

"I'll hammer them," Emily growled.

Despite all his worries, Papa had to smile. "Of course you will. But first, have some dinner." He draped the wet handkerchief over the knob of the front door. "I'm going to study now."

"Joan will bring you a plate," Mama said.

"I'll need some water, too," Papa said as he bounced

back to his feet. He bolted the door and then headed for the room he was using temporarily as a study.

Mama put her arms around us and ushered us down the hall. "Make sure you bring two cups of water to Papa," she instructed me. "One cup for drinking and one cup for his ink. I have a feeling he'll have to write a lot of poetry tonight."

Four

When we had finished our supper, we helped Mama unpack, which helped take our minds off the day's events.

There was something exciting about moving into a new house—as if we were explorers in a different country. And this house was more unusual than most, with high ceilings and walls with old, angular markings from the paintings, charts, and chalkboards they had once borne.

In the very front of the building, Papa had finished knocking together a crude counter, though the stenciled sides of the wooden scraps needed to be painted over, and there were shelves behind the counter. In the next room, Papa had already set up two ironing shelves out of wooden planks; and we got out the irons, the watering bottles, and the starch while Mama set up her pedal-run sewing machine.

The third room was for drying, so Papa had strung

clotheslines back and forth. There was more rope up than he had ever used in Ohio—as if he expected more laundry. Above the lines strung in even rows, far out of reach, was the tall ceiling with the molding. Desks and chalkboards had long since been carted away, but we could see the marks on the floors and the walls. And though the rooms had been washed and dusted, they still smelled of chalk and glue. A wood-burning stove squatted in one corner like a squat black bug. I supposed the school hadn't been fully converted to gas and the stove had been kept to heat the classroom in the winter. In Papa's methodical way, he had stacked kindling and wood beside it, ready to dry all the loads of laundry that would come.

The room next to the kitchen room was the washing room, where the wringing machine was already assembled. With a hammer, Mama opened the crate, and we unpacked the heavy laundry soap and the rest of our things. Then we ranged the washboards out like soldiers, preparing for the great battle the next day against the forces of filth. Papa had told me one time that the washboard was a Chinese invention that we had brought to America, though I don't know about that. Beneath the windows sat the row of big metal washtubs, gaping like so many empty frogs.

"Ah, here it is," Mama said. From one crate she brought out a small brass bell covered with flowery decorations and mottos in Chinese. We followed her in a procession back to the front door.

Papa had already prepared the hook over the doorway. I picked up Emily in my arms, and when Mama had given her the bell, Emily hung it up so that when the front door opened, it would make the bell ring. "Now we're really settled in," Emily said.

As the sun set, Mama began to turn on the gas jets in the house. They were little pipes that stuck out of the wall. When you lit them, the gas burned, giving off light.

In the kitchen next to the washing room, we finished

36

taking the rest of Mama's things out of the crates, including the rice and some salted vegetables. "Now we can eat real food tomorrow," Mama declared.

When we had done what we could downstairs, I got the bags that Emily and I had been carrying and took them upstairs.

Together, four of us put together the bed that Emily and I used and placed it next to the window. Our dresser was already there, with the cracked mirror in the frame above it. Next to it was a chair. In our old home, our things pretty well crammed the tiny room we had. But everything looked a bit lost in that classroom.

Mama sent Bobby off to bed while she and I helped Emily get into her nightclothes. As she brushed out Emily's hair, Mama turned Emily toward the gaslight and pointed meaningfully toward it. "Remember, play with the gas jet and the gas might come into the house and choke you or blow up the whole house—and you'll get back to Ohio even sooner than you want."

Then, as she put us to bed, she told us a couple of stories about children who had played with the gas jets and died particularly gruesome deaths.

As she tucked the quilt up around our necks, she looked down at Emily sternly. "And," she declared, "it all happened because bad, bad children disobeyed their parents." She stroked the hair out of Emily's eyes. "Now good night."

Mama went over to the gas jet and pointed at it again. "What did I say about these things when we lived in Ohio?" she asked Emily.

Emily would have kept a stubborn silence if I hadn't elbowed her. "Only you and Joan and Papa can turn it off," she mumbled.

With a nod of her head, Mama turned down the gas jet so that the light went out. When Mama was gone, I felt Emily's bony elbow in my side. "Joan?"

"What?" I mumbled sleepily.

Emily was lying on her side, looking at the wall where the gas jet was. "Do you think Mama would tell a fib?"

The pillow felt so soft at that moment that I just murmured, "She doesn't want you to play with the gas jets. Now good night."

As we lay there, I could hear the old building talking to itself. Out in the hallway, old boards creaked. Something rattled in a room below. The bed shook as Emily turned toward me for protection, but she took in her breath so sharply that I made the mistake of asking, "What's wrong?"

In the dim light coming in from the street, Emily's eyes looked very wide. "There's a tree. I can see its shadow on the shade. It's got these long, bony arms that are moving." She clutched at me. "I think it's trying to get us."

"Don't look at it, then." Putting a hand to her shoulder, I shoved her over onto her back. She lay there for a moment and then announced, "This is even worse. Now I can't see anything. I can just hear it." When the wind made the tree branches beat against the window, Emily scurried under the quilt. "Now it's trying to get us."

"Emily, come out of there before you suffocate." Exasperated, I tried to drag the quilt back down from her head.

Emily, though, had a death grip on it. "If there are any monsters there"—her voice came muffled through the quilt—"you want someone big like Joan and not someone small like me."

It took both hands, but I managed to get Emily's head back into the open air. "Now, no more shenanigans," I scolded her. "Go to sleep."

When I lay back down again, the pillow felt as soft as ever. But it wasn't too long before Emily poked me again. I tried to push her away without looking and waved my hand vaguely in the air. "Go away."

"I don't like it here," Emily insisted.

"That's nice," I murmured drowsily.

"This place is worse than a jail. It's a trap." I tried to ignore her, but every now and then these little pronouncements would spout from Emily. "I keep hearing the tree moving." A moment later: "It's coming in." And after a minute: "Joan-ee, I can't sleep."

"I can," I mumbled.

"I'm scared," she complained. "The tree's moving."

"It's just the wind," I muttered into my pillow.

Emily snuggled up against me. "It's going to get us."

Once Emily's imagination got going, it was hard to stop it. With a sigh, I rolled over onto my side to look at her, but Emily had buried her head underneath the quilt again. "No, the tree sounds just like the ocean."

Emily lowered the quilt to stare at me accusingly. "You've never been to the ocean."

"Neither have you, so how do you know it doesn't? Come on, we'll make like spoons." I rolled Emily over onto her side so that her back was to me. Then I held her against me tight. "If I tell you a story, will you let me sleep?"

"You're the best storyteller," Emily said, trying to butter me up.

I gave her a little shake. "Will you go to sleep?"

Emily started to lay out the conditions for the performance. "And I like the way you add all sorts of details and do different voices."

"Will you?" I demanded.

"Yes," she promised.

"A young farmer was walking along the road," I began.

"I like that one," Emily said. I knew she did because whenever Mama told it, she always fell asleep.

"It was late on a fine afternoon," I started again.

"A summer afternoon," she corrected me.

"It was late on a fine summer afternoon," I said, and Emily fitted herself contentedly against me from head to toe. "And he'd just been to a town and sold a basket of turnips."

39

"And he was going home," Emily prompted me.

I put my hand to her head and stroked her hair. "Hey, who's telling the story?" I teased.

"You are." Emily shifted her head to my arm, and I could feel her small body rise and fall as she breathed. She seemed to feel safe now in my arms. As Emily had told me one time, "You might be bossy, but you always make things okay."

As Emily lay there quietly, I found myself wishing that were true. "And he was going home when he heard a woman singing. He stopped dead in his tracks to listen because her song hung like a rainbow to the ears, a rainbow that glittered and twisted through the air like a snake dancing."

I kept my voice as gentle as my hand. In the mirror above the dresser, I could see Emily's eyelids begin to droop. "When the song ended, it almost broke his heart. 'No, don't stop,' he whispered. By now the sun had disappeared over the horizon, and the trees looked as black and massive as a wall of black iron."

Emily's eyes were closed, and so I kept my voice deliberately soft in the darkness. "As the moon rose slowly, the woman's voice soared in greeting, singing of riding the back of the wind all the way into the night sky where the stars wriggled and shimmered like schools of fish."

I closed my own eyes, feeling at peace. I forgot about the train ride and the man at the station and the men by the fence. "The moonbeams reached the forest by the road, so that the edges of the leaves were like silvery smiles, and the black branches seemed to wave and point to a narrow path. Still he hesitated by the road, for the forest was the sort of queer place where anything could happen and had happened."

As I spoke, I felt myself floating into the darkness just like the voice. . . .

He stood there uncertainly because he was a sensible man who always did the sensible thing. But then the beautiful

40

voice spoke of swimming through the night and gathering the glittering stars, and he knew he had to find the woman who sang of such things. So, taking a deep breath, he plunged off the road and down the dark, winding path.

Bushes grew around a little clearing on the banks of the stream, and he hid in their shadow as he peeked through the branches. There, standing in the open, were three women, their faces turned toward the moon as if they were drinking its light like wine. Each was lovely, but the loveliest was the singer herself.

They were dressed in silken gowns—though the farmer could not decide what color they were because they seemed to change every moment. Around the women's shoulders were cloaks of golden feathers that rippled with a soft light of their own like the sunlight on the surface of a pond.

Hardly daring to breathe, the farmer crouched in the dark forest as they danced to the one woman's triumphant song, sweeping their arms as if they were already in the night sky fishing for stars.

However, though it was dark, the night air was still muggy and uncomfortable. So the lovely singer suggested that they take off their cloaks because they were too hot; and the others were only too glad to shed the cloaks, which lay like piles of gold at their feet. Then, relieved of a hot, heavy burden, they moved with lighter, quicker steps.

Finally, when they were thirsty from the dancing and singing, the three turned to the stream. The farmer should have run away from the magical creatures, or he should have sat in the dark until they were gone. But the singing was so delightful that it had made him foolish—so foolish, in fact, that he not only stayed but did a terrible thing.

He crept out of the bushes and across the clearing. While the women's backs were turned, he snatched up the precious cloak of the lovely singer. It was still damp and warm from her dancing. Clutching it to his chest, he darted back among the bushes and hid it among the roots of a tall tree.

When the women turned around, the farmer strode boldly out of the bushes. Gazing only at the singer who had so enchanted him, he asked, "Please, what's your name?"

With sharp, frightened cries, though, the women instantly bent and snatched up their cloaks. Throwing them about their shoulders, they spread their arms and immediately changed into golden kingfishers that rose, darting and weaving, up the silver beams of moonlight.

All of them, that is, except the singer. "Wait, wait," she called and held up her cloakless arms toward the sky. But her sisters were now only distant black specks against the moon.

"I just want to talk," the farmer said desperately. "I don't mean you any harm."

Tears in her eyes, the singer turned. "If you speak the truth, let me leave."

However, now that she stood right before him, he knew he could not let her go. "If you marry me, I'll give it back to you."

"I'm a star fisher," she pleaded. "I belong in the sky."

Despite all her arguments, the farmer coaxed and begged her to marry him; and though she did not believe the farmer, it was her only hope, so the star fisher reluctantly agreed. She accompanied the farmer to his village, where her beauty caused all the other villagers to murmur in wonder.

When they were married, she pressed him for her cloak. "I'll give it back to you soon," he said guiltily. "Just stay with me a little longer."

Though she now trusted him even less than before, she had no choice. She lived with the farmer, but she no longer sang or danced. She did not even look up at the sky but always kept her eyes upon the ground. Instead, she searched for the cloak constantly. She hunted all around the house and in the fields and even left to go back to the forest clearing. However, her husband had already removed the cloak from the original spot and hidden it in a newer, better place.

Eventually, she bore the farmer a daughter. And at times during those years, the village would occasionally hear two birds singing sweet, lovely melodies at night. However, the birds did not sound like nightingales or any other birds the villagers had ever heard.

Ashamed, the farmer would cover his ears, for he knew they were his wife's sisters calling to her to return to them. There were times when he almost kept his promise and gave her back her cloak, but he would look at his wife and know that he could never willingly give her up.

And then one evening when the sisters began a sad tune, the infant daughter tottered outside in the courtyard to listen. Lifting her head, she began to sing with them.

Hastily the farmer hurried outside to quiet her, but she had already stopped to stare up at a golden feather drifting down. Laughing, she stretched one pudgy hand up for the shining feather; but she missed it, and instead it landed on her sleeve, where it instantly turned into a spot of blood. Frightened as much by the sight of blood as by the strangeness of the event, the girl began to scream in terror, waving her arm stiffly.

The farmer took the frightened child to their house, where his wife waited in the doorway. When she saw the spot of blood on her daughter's sleeve, she looked at the farmer and saw that he understood also: her sisters had marked the child as a star fisher.

Even so, the years went on. Her sisters sang, the farmer made promises, the star fisher hunted, and their daughter grew.

She could sing and dance, and in her the farmer found the sweet delight he had lost in her mother. And the farmer, afraid of the other star fishers, always kept his daughter close

43

to home. If she ventured outside under her father's watchful eye, the other villagers avoided the half-magical child, whispering and pointing at her.

"I don't belong here," she had once complained to her mother.

"Neither of us does," her mother had sighed.

Finally the star fisher saw her chance and asked her daughter to play a game with her father; and when she cheerfully agreed, the star fisher coached her carefully on what she was to do.

That evening, she sang and danced in the courtyard for her father, as had become their custom; but after a while she stopped. When their father asked her what was wrong, she pretended to be frightened, saying that her mother had said she was going to leave him that evening.

His eyes automatically went to a pile of rice straw, but just as quickly he looked back at his daughter and assured her that her mother was only making a bad joke.

As she had been directed, she dutifully told her mother where her father had looked. That very evening, when he was asleep, the star fisher went to the heap of straw. With quiet desperation, she searched through the straw and then with her fingers clawed at the dirt beneath. There, sealed inside a box, was her magical cloak.

As she held it up, the feathers glimmered in the moonlight as if finally waking after all these years. And the light woke her family, as it did all the villagers.

As her daughter stumbled sleepily into the courtyard, the star fisher turned triumphantly. "I'll come back for you."

"No, please, don't go," the farmer begged as he ran out into the courtyard.

The star fisher, though, simply threw the cloak about her shoulders and raised her arms skyward. In the wink of an eye, she had changed into a golden kingfisher that circled joyfully up toward the moon.

"Wait, wait," the farmer said as he held out his arms after her.

But the bird only soared higher until she vanished from sight. And suddenly, from deep within the night sky, her sisters welcomed her gleefully in song.

The villagers heard the birds only one other time, and that was when the mother returned for her daughter. And though the mother never came back, the daughter could sometimes be seen overhead at night, golden feathers shining in the moonlight as she glided over the long, winding Milky Way, skimming up the stars like a kingfisher scooping up a beakful of tiny, shining fish. And then, her body glowing with stars, she would sweep across the black sky like a fiery comet, back and forth, back and forth. . . .

Outside our window, the tree was still rustling. "I can hear the tree," Emily said sleepily, "but it doesn't sound scary anymore. It sounds just like the wind . . . through wings."

I said very softly, "And the star fisher would stretch her wings and let the wind lift her up, higher and higher, on and on . . . like an endless river flowing toward the moon. . . ."

And it was around then that Emily began to snore.

Five

*W*e woke up when we heard the hoe scratching the dirt. Since Mama always got up early, I figured it had to be her. Emily yawned and then clacked her teeth together. "Why is Mama digging so early?"

"Who knows?" I nudged my little sister. "Come on. Get up." But Emily merely pressed her face into the pillow and tried to sleep some more. The pillow was feeling so soft and warm that I would have liked to have gone back to bed, too; but I kept hearing that persistent scratching noise—like a big chicken clawing the ground for worms. Scrape. Scrape. Scrape.

So I slipped out of bed—but that floor was cold—and wound up walking on tippy-toe over to the window. Taking a corner of the old window shade, I raised it to peek out. Down below I could see Miss Lucy in a plain gingham dress and a kerchief tied up around her head as she chopped viciously at a weed. "Miss Lucy gets up earlier than Mama."

Her curiosity aroused, Emily burrowed out of the quilt and crawled on her knees to the edge of the bed so she could look out with me. Then she plopped backward on the bed. "Then I'd better sleep for the both of them."

Getting Emily up was like trying to push a slow freight train up a hill. Seizing her wrists, I dragged her up into a sitting position. "Come on. You don't want to be late for school, do you?"

"Sure," she mumbled and would have flopped back down if I'd let her. Already next door I could hear Bobby banging around as he got ready.

She sat like a little doll with half-closed eyes while I combed out her hair and braided it. Hastily I put my own hair into practical pigtails and got dressed. Emily tried—I'll give her that much. However, by the time I was finished, she'd only managed to put her head and one arm into her dress.

Frustrated, I stuffed my feet into my shoes and had just finished lacing them when Mama called out, "Joan, come down here."

"I'm dressing Emily," I shouted back. I managed to find her other arm, bent like a bird's wing inside her dress; and between the two of us we got it through the proper sleeve. Straightening her clothes hastily, I banged on the wall. "Bobby," I yelled, "help Emily with her shoes."

Then I went down the steps two at a time to see what Mama wanted.

She was in the kitchen, where she had laid out some pennies all in a row. "Buy something to make sandwiches for lunch," she said. Though Mama was not particularly taken with American bread, she had quickly seen its usefulness in making quick meals.

I swept the coins into one palm. "That's barely enough for a loaf, Mama."

Mama was trying to distract herself from her worries by polishing the stove. "I know, but we haven't had any customers yet and the move took most of our money."

I heard the sound of Miss Lucy's hoe outside. "Couldn't we borrow from Miss Lucy?"

"Your father is a proud, learned man," Mama insisted. "We don't borrow."

I figured out what Mama was really up to. Mama was too ashamed to go herself, so she was sending me. "Why do I have to go, Mama?"

Mama straightened as if I'd just smacked her. "Because I tell you," she scolded me. "At home, a girl does what she's told."

I know it sounds silly, but I think at that moment I saw my mother for the first time, not as the all-powerful woman who could handle anything but as a human being: a small, frightened, vulnerable woman alone in a strange land, except for her not-always-too-grateful family. And knowing that Mama did not have magical powers made me feel grown-up and sad and angry all at once.

I should have kept my mouth shut, but I couldn't help blurting out, "We're in America, Mama."

"And you're getting just as spoiled and just as lazy as an American brat," Mama snapped.

The pennies were tight in my fist. "That's not fair, Mama. We have more chores than the American children."

Mama reared back indignantly. "Don't you talk back to me."

Mama and I might still have been arguing, but Papa heard us and came in that moment in an athletic shirt and pants. "Can I have some tea, Mama?"

Glad of the excuse, Mama turned her back to me. It was a view that I got to see often enough. Papa took me by the shoulders and turned me around. "Now, don't go giving your mama a hard time. She's got enough to worry about. And

48

anyway," he scolded me gently, "we don't want to fight on our first week in our new home; we might have bad luck. Just go get the bread."

It was hard to refuse Papa. I began feeling so guilty that I gave up any pretense of pride. With my lips pressed tightly together, I barged out of the kitchen; but as I stalked down the hallway, I kept muttering, "It's not fair. It's not fair."

I slammed the front door so Mama would know just how angry I felt. Outside, children were already trudging up the street toward school and men and women were bustling toward work. They glanced at me curiously, but today my anger was my armor against their looks and I ignored them.

The store was already open. A huge sign over the store front proclaimed to the whole world that it was Edward Edgar's Emporium. The store had a little bit of everything from pairs of shoes to some shirts, bolts of cloth, jars of penny candy that made my mouth water, and all sorts of canned goods on shelves on the wall.

Behind a counter was a man with long hair in a white shirt and tie, and over his pants he wore an apron. Black garters held up his sleeves. _"Howdy, honey,"_ he said brightly. _"You want some more crackers for your soup?"_

I looked longingly at the candy and forced myself to take my eyes away. _"No, sir, I'd like some bread."_

"Right." He wrote it down so he wouldn't forget. His pencil poised over the pad. _"And what else?"_

Shamefaced, I noticed a sign on the counter and saw that the bread would take most of my money. _"I have to think."_

"Got some nice cheese, sugar." Mr. Edgar set a loaf down upon the counter top and started to turn to some foil-wrapped cheese. _"How much would you like?"_

Fortunately, I saw the price. _"No, cheese makes my little sister sick,"_ I fibbed.

Mr. Edgar began to tap his fingers on the counter top while I desperately tried to come up with a solution. The

49

problem was that there was none. The tins of beef were out of the question, and so were any other cuts of meat in the store. Even the bacon—if we could have cooked it okay—would still have cost too much.

I turned slowly until I saw the vegetables sitting in a row, each in their own basket with a little sign fixed to the front. The only thing we could afford was a head of lettuce. *"I'll have some lettuce."*

"Right," Mr. Edgar said and wrote that down, too. His pencil poised over the pad. *"And what else?"*

"That's it."

He scratched the tip of his ear with the end of the pencil. *"No tomatoes? No cucumbers?"*

"No." I kept my eyes right on the counter as I began to count out the coins.

"That's too plain an order for a salad," he sighed.

"We use the lettuce a lot in cooking," I lied.

"Do tell? I'd like the recipe sometime." Mr. Edgar held up the pad and pointed his pencil at the price, waiting for me to pay.

The blood rushed to my face. I wished it were Mama or even Bobby going through this humiliation—not me. Slowly I opened my hand, wishing each second that I could shrink small enough to crawl under one of Mr. Edgar's baskets.

As I counted out the pennies, he shook his head. *"What was on your mother's mind? She should've given you more than that."* He picked up the loaf. *"Tell you what. Why don't you buy some nice apples instead? Nourishing and healthy, and if there's a worm,"*—he winked—*"you even get a bit of meat thrown in for free."*

But it would be obvious to our schoolmates how poor we were if we just ate apples. I wanted our family to make a good impression on their first day.

"Apples, worms, meat," he repeated hopefully. When I still didn't say anything, he complained in an aggrieved tone,

"I don't think anyone in town would know a joke if they tripped over it."

I smiled hastily. *"Oh, yes, I get it now. I'd like the bread and the lettuce."*

Mr. Edgar scratched the tip of his nose. *"Tell you what. You look like you have an honest face. I bet it runs in the family. Why don't you ask your father to come over? I could give him a little credit."*

However, I knew Mama was right: being a laundryman was bad enough for him, but being a poor laundryman was even worse. I began to rummage around in the basket. *"No, sir. We don't believe in credit."* Selecting a head of lettuce, I brought it over to the counter top.

"Hope your rabbit likes its meal," Mr. Edgar said, wrapping the lettuce and the bread in a brown paper bag.

"Rabbit?"

He sighed. *"It's another joke."*

"Oh, yes, of course." When I slid the rest of the pennies onto the counter, I saw that I had been holding them so tightly that they had left the imprint of little round circles on my hand—like the suckers of an octopus I had seen once in a fish market.

Handing the bag to me, he nodded his head in a kindly manner. *"You keep what I said in mind. Mention it to your father."*

Cheeks burning red, I thanked Mr. Edgar and hurried out of the store.

Mama was still in the kitchen when I got back to the laundry. "Well?" she asked.

I set the bag down on the table and looked at her accusingly. "I got the bread."

Mama came over curiously. "And . . . ?"

I rubbed at my palm. The impression left by the pennies was still there. "I got what we could afford."

Opening the bag, Mama peered inside. "Lettuce?"

"That was it," I declared. It was like being a crewman on a boat just about to sink—even though it would be a disaster for me, there was some satisfaction in knowing that the captain was going down, too.

However, I should have known Mama better. Mama took out the loaf and the head of lettuce. "Well, it's still more than I had back in China. We'll make lettuce sandwiches."

While Mama washed the lettuce, I found a knife and cut thick slabs of bread. It smelled almost fresh-baked, as if Mr. Edgar had gotten it that very morning.

We had just put the sandwiches into the paper bags when Bobby and Emily came into the kitchen. "This is important," Mama warned them. "When you eat lunch, make sure you eat separately."

Bobby looked at Mama as if she'd just told him to fly to the moon. "Why?"

Emily was already suspicious. Peeking inside one bag, she lifted the top piece of bread. "Where's the sandwich?" she demanded. "There's only lettuce."

"It's a lettuce sandwich." Mama shoved her hand away and closed the bag again. "It's good for you."

"It's rabbit food," Bobby said indignantly.

"Rabbits are very healthy animals," Mama argued. "It's either lettuce sandwiches or empty air."

Bobby and Emily each gave a grudging hug to Mama and stepped outside, where I could hear them greeting Miss Lucy. But Mama just kept her hands folded in front of her when I picked up my lunch and stepped out to her. "You're the oldest, so you have to set the example."

"I'll try," I said.

"Don't try; just do it." Mama finally gave me a hug, but I didn't return it because I still hadn't forgiven her for making me do all the dirty work that morning.

Six

On the brow of the hill sat the high school, a big, three-story brick building surrounded by a large field and basketball courts. Emily and Bobby's grammar school began a little farther back, but it was almost the twin to the high school — as if they had both been built at about the same time.

"We'll meet there at lunchtime," I said, pointing to the fence that separated the two schools.

With a final wave to Emily, I joined the river of boys and girls heading into the high school, where I stood uncertainly for a moment. To my left, I saw a tall stork of a girl talking animatedly with two shorter girls who reminded me of pet poodles. *"Did you get permission to go on the choir trip to Washington?"* one of the smaller girls was asking.

The tall girl shook her head, her blond bangs drifting

back and forth across her forehead. *"I'm still working on my mother."*

I walked over to them. *"Excuse me,"* I said. *"Do you know where the principal's office is?"*

They eyed me with a curiosity that was not unfriendly, and the tall girl stretched out an arm to point. *"Down that hallway and to the left."*

Encouraged, I lingered on. *"My name's Joan. Joan Lee."*

"Havana Garret," the tall girl said and nodded to one of the shorter girls, who had a mass of brown sausage curls. *"And that's Henrietta Deems."* She indicated a girl whose black hair had been pulled back into a bun and decorated with a red bow. *"And that's Florie Adams."*

"Havana is an unusual name," I said.

"Yes" was Havana's curt answer, and then she was turning anxiously back toward Florie. *"I've tried just about everything to make her let me go."*

"You know we have to turn in the signed permission notes in two days," Florie pointed out. *"My mother said I couldn't go unless you and Henrietta went."*

"Same here," Henrietta chimed in.

I stood there for a moment, wondering if I had offended Havana by asking so bluntly about her name; but she and her friends were engaged in such a heated conversation that I was afraid to interrupt. Instead, I waited for some natural break in the conversation or for them to notice me again. However, either they were caught up in their problem or they were determined to ignore me, because they didn't so much as glance my way.

"Well, good-bye," I said. No one acknowledged my existence as I made my way to the principal's office. It was small, with frosted panes of glass and wood paneling. Books and hats lay piled on the shelves, and there were layers of papers on her desk like the layers of a giant sandwich.

In the center of the chaos was a stern-looking, middle-aged woman in a white blouse and long black skirt. She was broad, but not fat—like an overstuffed sofa standing on two legs—and her hair had been done up in a series of buns like layers of a cake. *"You must be one of Miss Lucy's new tenants,"* she said.

I supposed there weren't any secrets in a small town. *"Yes, ma'am."*

"I'm Miss Blake." Bidding me take a seat, she plunged her hand directly into the center of the mess upon her desk and extracted a file with the necessary form.

In a polite but brisk manner, she helped me fill out the form. *"Now, where in China were you born?"*

"Actually," I said almost apologetically, *"I was born in Lima,"* and added, *"Ohio, not Peru."*

She smiled patiently as if she had already figured that out. *"Really? That accounts for your English. I had cousins up there working in the locomotive factories."* She handed me the form. *"Can you fill out the rest of this yourself?"*

"Of course," I said and took the pen from her.

She watched as I wrote down my birthdate. *"So you're fifteen."*

"Yes, ma'am," I said, feeling as if this were some sort of unofficial test.

She watched the pen scratch its way across the page. *"We don't get to see many Chinese women coming in."*

I frowned as I tried to read and hold a conversation at the same time. *"My father is a scholar, and I think there's an exemption for them."* I shrugged. *"I know there's one for merchants."*

Miss Blake looked puzzled. *"Is he going to open up a school?"*

She was just being curious, I suppose. But I felt almost as if I were being interrogated. *"No, ma'am. We have a laundry."*

Miss Blake smiled primly. *"Then he's not really a scholar."*

I slapped my pencil down so I could defend my father.

"Yes be is." I was so annoyed that I began to fib. *"He's a very learned scholar, in fact."*

"Indeed." She sniffed and turned to get a blank sheet of paper. *"Now, what courses did you take?"*

"Geometry," I said, *"and biology."* And I named my other courses. *"You should be getting a transcript shortly."*

"Indeed," Miss Blake said and settled back in her chair. *"And just what do you intend to do when you graduate from here?"*

Both Papa and Mama made noises about going back to China, but that event seemed as remote as Judgment Day. *"I'm going to go on to college."*

"Indeed." She looked at me as if I had just said I wanted to be the Queen of England.

I felt that I ought to justify myself. *"I want to learn."*

"Indeed."

"I do," I asserted.

"Indeed."

As I worked on the form, she finished a list of my classrooms; and when I was finished, she gave me something for my parents to sign. *"If they can't sign their names, Miss Lucy can help them."*

She acted as if we were fresh off the boat, and that attitude annoyed me. *"They can sign,"* I assured her.

With a military stride, Miss Blake led me from the office and down a long hallway with a brown linoleum floor, past a display case for trophies, though there were only a few. Pausing by the door of one classroom, she knocked.

"Come in," a woman said.

Beckoning me to follow her, Miss Blake opened the door and swept into a large room with wooden walls on which hung big black chalkboards and a large map of Italy. Sunlight streamed in through the large frame windows onto desks made of wood and cast iron painted black. Each desk was fastened to wooden boards like a squat skier.

As Miss Blake strode into the classroom, all the pupils

rose to their feet with a sound of thunder. _"Good morning, Miss Blake,"_ the class said with one voice.

Miss Blake ignored them as she went to the teacher standing with a blue book in her hand. The teacher was as skinny as Miss Blake was broad, with a long jaw and blond hair piled upward into a cone that made her seem even taller. Though she seemed only in her twenties, she looked just as tough as Miss Blake.

"This is Joan Lee," Miss Blake said. _"She's one of Miss Lucy's new neighbors."_ In a small town, that seemed enough of an explanation—as if they knew already about the laundry.

The teacher scrutinized me. _"How do you do? I'm Miss Sims."_ She went to a cabinet and got a textbook. _"If you'll stop by here after school, I'll give you a list of make-up assignments."_ Half turning, she looked at the classroom and pointed to an empty desk in front of a red-haired girl in a navy middy blouse that was starched to a uniform sharpness. _"You can sit in front of Bernice."_ I saw a few of the girls smirk at that, though I couldn't see why.

As Miss Blake left and Miss Sims went on with an English lesson, I went down the aisle. But all I could really see were eyes: twenty-three pairs of eyes watching me as if I were trying to walk along a tightrope rather than a floor.

When Bernice grinned a welcome at me, it made all the freckles on her cheeks rise up like a flock of birds. Nervously I tried to smile back as I slid in. The top of my desk had a long, thin little trough for pencils and pens, and on the right side was a hole with a metal base where I could put an ink bottle.

I did my best to take notes, but I'm afraid that I paid more attention to the other pupils than to Miss Sims. I was glad to notice that they weren't dressed any too differently from the students in the school I had left—except that the girls seemed to fancy little pins: sailboats, flowers, and so on. And the boys didn't have their hair slicked back. I attributed that to the difference in tastes between regions. I figured that I could work up some pin at home—Bobby was clever with a knife and a piece of wood. So I began drawing designs on my pad of paper rather than taking notes.

I was relieved to see that the class was discussing a Shakespeare play that we had already read in my old school. The smart thing to do was keep quiet, watch the others, and do as they did. As Papa was fond of saying, "The nail that sticks out gets hammered."

"Now," Miss Sims asked, *"what does the 'wherefore' in 'Wherefore art thou Romeo?' mean?"* She nodded to a brunette with sausage curls. *"Ann?"*

Ann bit her lip. *"She wants to know where he is?"*

"That's what everyone thinks," Miss Sims said and began to survey the room for someone else to call on.

My hand shot up. And when Miss Sims nodded toward me, I answered, *"Juliet is asking why he has to be called Romeo Montague. Why couldn't he be a Smith?"*

"Exactly," Miss Sims said.

It was nice, for a change, to do something right and have it acknowledged. At home, we could work all day, do everything we were supposed to do, and not get one word of praise. We never heard what we did right, only what we did wrong. I don't think Mama and Papa knew what a compliment was — at least with their children.

Ann, though, turned and shot a look at me that was pure poison. She obviously didn't like being shown up, but I just shrugged.

I didn't think anything about it until the next period, which was physical education. In the locker room, the other girls changed into dark blue blouses and balloon-like pants called bloomers. It was similar to the outfit I'd had to wear in Ohio, so I could bring it the next day. Fortunately, the physical education teacher, Miss Armstrong, had an extra one I could borrow for that day.

As we were changing, Ann glanced at me. *"You're a little dark, aren't you?"*

I blinked, looking down at the back of my hand, and suddenly realized that she wasn't referring to my tan but to my skin color. _"You're a little pale, aren't you?"_ I shot back.

Ann jumped to her feet. _"Miss Armstrong better burn that suit after you use it."_

I balled my hands into fists when Miss Armstrong thrust herself between us. _"We don't tolerate that kind of talk in this school. One more peep from you, Ann Wood, and I'll turn you over to Miss Blake."_

Ann grew even paler at the thought of the principal. _"Yes, ma'am."_

Miss Armstrong shoved Ann toward the gymnasium. _"You can take out your energy in the gymnasium."_ She nodded to me. _"You too, Joan."_

Ann was waiting for me by the doorway as I left the locker room. As I crossed the threshold, she stuck out a foot and tripped me. _"You poor dear, a little slow on your feet this morning."_ She reached down to help me up.

"I can do it myself," I said and shook her off.

Miss Armstrong saw only the final part of our little scene. _"What you two need to learn is a little teamwork."_ She was dressed in a larger size of our gymnasium clothes except for the big silver whistle around her neck. Reaching for it now, she blew on it loudly. _"Volleyball, everyone."_

Our physical education teacher made a point of putting Ann and me on the same team. I think it was her idea to have us work together; but what it did was give Ann golden opportunities to slide up and bump, shove, and even trip me, until by the end of the period I got so mad that I wound up throwing the volleyball at Ann.

The instructor's whistle pierced the noise in the gymnasium. She grabbed me by the collar, lifting me slightly off the floor. _"That will be enough of that. You are to write two hundred times, 'I will be a good sport.' And I want that by tomorrow."_

Behind her, Ann made a face at me.

I was still limping at lunchtime as I moved toward the fence separating the grammar school playground from the high school. Bobby, a natural athlete, was already playing baseball with the other boys in his class.

Emily was off in another part of the playground, skipping rope with some of the other girls in her class. I recognized the chant they were using as one of Emily's — she was the creative one.

I stood by the fence, wanting to call them over to have lunch with me; but they were doing so well, I knew I should leave them alone.

I sat down by myself, feeling ugly and stupid and lonely. The more I saw of West Virginia, the more I wished I were back in Ohio.

What I hated most was that I felt so awkward — the worst thing was my hands. I didn't know what to do with them. Should I leave them at my sides? Should I clasp them behind my back? Should I fold them in front of me?

Opening my pad of paper, I began writing down the punishment assignment to occupy my mind until Emily and Bobby were ready to eat lunch. Suddenly, as I sat with my own thoughts, I felt a shadow across my face, and I glanced up to see Bernice.

Mama wouldn't worry about her posture. Her spine was as straight as a pole and she held up her head with what the magazines called a ladylike elegance. She spoke slowly, almost with a self-conscious diction. *"May I eat with you?"*

The *"yes"* was almost on my lips when I remembered our lunches. *"I'm sorry. I . . . I promised to eat with my brother and sister."*

Bernice started to sit down anyway. *"I can wait with you until they come."*

I put my hand on her hip to stop her. *"They're the shy type. They might not come over."*

Bernice froze there in a half crouch, her head swiveling around to look at the grammar school playground. I looked in the same direction and saw the same thing she did: the small Chinese boy and girl playing with the others and generally presenting the opposite picture of being shy.

I braced myself for some storm of accusations, but Bernice just pressed her lips together primly. *"Oh. So I see."*

I almost relented. But Bernice might shame our family in front of the entire school, and from the school it would spread over the whole town. It didn't matter about me; however, Bernice could ruin everything for Bobby and Emily. Agonized, I knew I couldn't even explain my reasons at all.

"I'm sorry," I said, grasping the bag.

"Of course," Bernice said gravely—as if she were twenty years older. *"I understand."*

"Understand what?" I asked, puzzled.

"You will never be accepted by the others if you're seen with me." I watched her retrace her steps across the field. The funny thing was that she didn't go over to the benches where the other girls sat chattering away as brightly as sparrows. Instead, she sat down on the concrete steps and began to eat by herself.

Despite Mama's warning, I was feeling so curious that I almost went over to eat with her; but at that moment Bobby and Emily showed up on the other side of the fence, both of them red-faced and out of breath from playing. "Who were you talking to, Joan?" Bobby asked. "She looks like a girl in my class."

"It could be a sister," I answered as he plopped down. "What do you know about her?"

"Not much." Bobby crunched his sandwich noisily. "Everybody avoids the girl in my class."

Emily had the more spectacular imagination. "I bet they're tied up in a feud."

Bobby had all the superior knowledge of his extra two

61

years. *"Don't be a goose. They live in town. Feuds are up in the hills."*

Emily corrected him. *"In a hollow."*

"They say it 'holler,'" Bobby corrected her back.

"Holl-er-r-r." Emily caressed the word against the roof of her mouth.

"And 'crick' for 'creek,'" Bobby said.

"Never mind," I said, staring down at my sandwich.

"How was your day, Joan?" Emily asked. "I've made two new friends."

For her sake, I smiled. "That's nice. So have I."

Emily opened her lunch bag without thinking and reached inside. When she raised the sandwich into the open, she looked disappointed. "Oh, I forgot." The sandwich sagged in one dirty fist as she looked through the mesh at me. "Rabbit food is rabbit food." However, she ate her sandwich anyway with loud crunching noises. "I'm going to have supper at Janey's house."

"Were you invited?" With Emily, you could never be sure.

"I will be," she asserted.

Bobby dusted off his hands after finishing his sandwich. "Don't be a pig. What about Mama and Papa?"

"That will leave more for them," Emily argued, but she spoke in a small voice as if she already knew that was a feeble excuse.

"I'll eat at home," Bobby promised.

"All right." Emily dipped her head reluctantly. "I will, too." She began looking around the playground for her friends. "Maybe Janey has an apple or something she can spare."

When Bobby started to wad up his paper bag, I pointed at it urgently. "Save it."

Sheepishly Bobby unfolded the ball of paper he had made out of his lunch bag and folded it carefully. Emily simply slapped it flat and began to shove it through one of the spaces in the mesh. "Here. You keep it for me."

I took it and began to fold it carefully while an impatient Bobby just shoved his through another space and let it flutter to the grass. "Race you," he shouted to Emily.

I snatched up Bobby's just before the wind sent it swirling away. And as I sat folding up old paper bags, I could hear the laughter and happy shouts all around me; and I felt as if I were trapped inside some glass cage—cut off from the laughter and happy voices that surrounded me.

Though the textbooks were different from those in Ohio, the subject matter was pretty much the same, so it wasn't really a question of catching up with the rest of the classes—only of doing the make-up assignments to show that I knew the material.

I felt as if the only people who approved of me were my teachers, so for the rest of the day I went on answering questions. And for the rest of the day, I could hear whisperings and gigglings wherever I went. Apparently the whole school had heard of the know-it-all girl. And since I detested whiny people, I hated myself even more for feeling sorry for myself.

I suppose when the star fisher's daughter had gone for a walk in their village, the neighbors had smirked in just the same way. Moving through the hallways, I felt as if I were marked by a drop of blood from a falling feather.

So you can't imagine what relief I felt when I heard the final bell ring that meant I was free. I got the lists of make-up assignments from my teachers—who, like Miss Sims, had prepared them by the end of the day. As I started to leave school with a pile of books, I saw Bernice's familiar erect spine ahead of me. _"Do you want to walk together?"_ I asked.

However, Bernice kept on moving out of the school.

"Bernice," I said in a louder voice.

She turned slowly as if puzzled that anyone would call her, and then she saw me. _"Hello,"_ she said timidly.

I tried to grin as I repeated, *"Do you want to walk together?"*

Bernice looked pretty when she smiled. *"That would be nice."*

"I hope you don't mind if my little brother and sister come along." I began to walk out the door.

Bernice waited for me to join her, her books held against her stomach. Each of them had been covered in brown paper, and on the face of each was the subject and her own address neatly inked in. *"I have a sister myself,"* she said.

As Ann and another girl passed by, they glanced at us. *"It figures,"* one of them said. And the other put her fingers in front of her mouth and tittered—something I'd never seen anyone do before.

I turned, puzzled, to Bernice, who was biting her lip. *"What do you think they meant?"*

Bernice shook her head. *"Folks in this town are terribly clannish. We moved into town ten years ago, and we're still treated like strangers."*

"Where do you come from?" I asked, because her accent didn't sound like that of the others.

"On my father's side, Boston." Bernice waved a hand vaguely toward the east while clutching her books. *"But my grandmother moved into this area a while back. Her third husband's family was involved in oil. He did not leave her much more than a house, though."*

Like everyone else, Bernice was disappointed to hear that we had come from an ordinary place like Ohio and not China. Whenever it happened, I felt like the star fisher's daughter, on the one hand belonging to an ordinary world, and belonging to a strange, exotic world, too—and one that I knew nothing about.

"But our parents are from China," I added hopefully. I just prayed that she didn't ask me any questions about that country because I knew as little as she did.

However, Bernice looked at me now as if she suspected that I was playing some trick on her. Even though we went on chatting innocently enough, I could tell that Bernice was nervous about something. Being surrounded by all the other pupils made her almost as uncomfortable as me . . . or maybe it was being seen with me.

Bobby and Emily were waiting by the gates to the high school. Emily's belly bulged suspiciously, as if she had something stored away under her sweater—whatever she could scavenge from her new friends. _"What took you so long?"_

I ignored her rudeness and nodded toward Bernice. _"This is my friend Bernice."_

Bobby was lounging against the gate as if he had no bones. _"Josephine's sister?"_

"Yes," Bernice declared brightly.

"This is Bobby," I said to Bernice, and indicated my little sister. _"And this is Emily."_

"Howdy-do," Emily said.

Bobby wasn't being any different from the other boys, but Mama would never accept that posture. Taking him by his collar, I pulled him upright. _"How did your day go? Did you have any . . . trouble?"_ I selected the word carefully because there were still other students around us.

When I finished the introductions, someone giggled behind me. Bernice stiffened and I whirled around, but the three girls behind us were watching the antics of a little dog across the street in someone's front yard. By now I was so sensitive to the sound of laughing that I was beginning to think that I was the target of it all.

"What's wrong?" Bobby asked.

"Nothing," I lied.

Bernice, though, had gotten a funny look on her face. _"Maybe we shouldn't walk home."_

I could feel my face reddening as I thought, She doesn't want to be seen with me. However, I kept control of myself.

"Maybe not," I said and forced myself to shrug as if I didn't care.

Bernice stared at me, hurt—I didn't know why. After all, she was the one who had made the suggestion. *"I was thinking that you might like to look at my notes on some of the courses. Perhaps . . . we could do some homework together later tonight?"* she asked in a small voice.

I thought it was a little odd considering that she didn't want to be seen walking with me, so I refused politely. *"Thank you, but we have chores."* She looked so disappointed that I added, *"But why don't you give me your address?"* I peered at the address on one of her books.

"Oh, no," she said quickly, covering it up. *"I meant at the library."*

"Maybe so," I said, not really understanding why she was afraid to walk with me but was willing to be seen with me at the library.

"Very well." Pivoting on her heel, she plunged down the hill, shoes slapping the pavement.

As I watched her back recede down the hill, Bobby scratched his head. "What was that all about?"

"Come on. Let's go home."

But as I walked, I couldn't help remembering the story from last night. I wondered if the star fisher's daughter had felt just as lonely in her village.

Seven

*T*he laundry bell tinkled as the door swung in. To my surprise, Papa was sitting at the front counter instead of Mama. Usually Papa took care of the heavy work in back, leaving Mama to wait on the customers.

"Oh," he said in disappointment when he saw us. "How was school?"

"Fine," Emily said quickly.

No matter what Papa thought of American schools, he wanted to be sure we had learned something that day, so he usually asked a lot of questions. But instead, Papa said, "That's good," lifted one of his philosophy books, and began to read.

Bobby scratched his head in surprise and looked back at us. I just raised my eyebrows and leaned my head to the side. "What do you want us to do, Papa?" Bobby asked.

"There's nothing for you to do." Papa kept his nose carefully buried in his book.

We blinked at one another because that was even odder. There were always chores. "There must be something for us to do," I objected.

Papa cleared his throat behind his book. "There weren't any customers."

We could all sense a major catastrophe about to happen. It must have been like this for a sailor on the *Titanic*, seeing the huge iceberg coming toward the ship.

"Where's Mama?" I asked.

"In back doing some figuring," Papa said. That was serious. It suggested that Mama was already trying to estimate how long we could keep the laundry afloat.

Emily crowded up to the counter. "What about all those dirty shirts you heard?"

Papa flicked a page over. "They must not have been talking Chinese."

Poor Papa. He was always such a dreamer. In his own way, he was always reaching for the stars—first the government exams, then America, and now the laundry. "They'll come, Papa," I said.

"Of course," Papa said and determinedly turned another page. I think he was so worried that he was not really reading. He was just turning the pages. "Now go and do your homework."

"And when it's finished?" Bobby asked carefully.

"You can go play," Papa said.

Bobby lingered. "May I have supper at a friend's house?"

"Yes," Papa snapped in exasperation. "Just be back before sunset."

"Okay." Bobby tore around the counter and thundered up the steps.

Feeling betrayed by Bobby, I pulled Emily away from the counter. "Come on. We'll play after we finish our homework."

Emily wrinkled up her nose. "You never want to play with me anymore."

I tapped her nose. "Well, I do today." In fact, it would be nice to pretend to be Emily's age again.

Emily, though, hesitated as if she'd swallowed a squirrel and it was now squirming around inside her. "Actually," she said slowly, "Janey's invited me to supper, too."

I was feeling spiteful. "Well, ask Papa, then."

However, before Emily could even open her mouth, Papa rattled his paper-covered book. "Yes."

If I had truly wanted to be mean, I could have insisted that they ask Mama, because I knew she would say no. But even at that moment, I wasn't totally heartless.

As we stumped up the steps, Emily suggested anxiously, "Maybe we ought to pray for rain and hope for lots of mud. Or maybe we ought to ask our friends to bring their laundry here."

My hand slid up the banister railing as I climbed. "That's too much like begging."

Bobby was already lying prone on the floor of our room as he did his homework. I did my homework and some of my make-up assignments—and also sat on Emily and Bobby to make sure they did theirs. In Emily's case, I quite literally plopped down on her.

"No," I said to her, "you can't go out to play until you finish one of your make-up assignments, too."

Emily squirmed underneath me. Outside our window, we could see how bright and sunny it was. "But Janey was going to take me down to the crick if there was time. I don't have to turn in the make-up assignments yet."

"You'll do them now," I argued. When Emily wanted to be slippery, it was like trying to ride a whirlwind.

"You're just jealous 'cause I've got friends, and you haven't got any," Emily shot back angrily.

That stung more than I liked. Sitting up, I rolled off. "All right. Go."

Emily sat up. "I didn't mean to say that."

"Yes you did. Now go." I gave her a shove that sent her sprawling on her back.

"There'll be other days." Emily squeezed me. "You're my best friend."

I swung out my elbows so that I could break her hold. "I don't want your pity."

The one thing about Emily is that she would be immediately sorry when she knew she had gone too far. "Besides, I need your help on the arithmetic." She began to hunt in her book bag for another pencil. "Won't you help me?"

No matter how irritated and hurt I felt, old habits died hard. "All right. But I have work of my own."

Bobby was the first to finish; and, after showing me two make-up assignments as well as all his homework, he raced out of the laundry before Mama could catch him and make him stay.

Emily, though, wasn't much longer than Bobby. "Finished," she cried and started to get up. She added, "And I did three make-up assignments, too."

Maliciously I pulled her back down. "Check your answers."

Grumbling, Emily sat down and her eyes raced over the pages of homework and make-up assignments. "It's okay," she announced the next second.

Feeling tired, I figured it was on her head if she failed. I concentrated on the sheet of paper in front of me. "Goodbye, then."

Emily jumped to her feet and started out, but she paused in the doorway. "I'll bring back something for you, Joan," she promised.

I looked up angrily. "What am I? Your pet dog?"

"Be that way." Emily sniffed and tossed her head. I heard her stomping down the hallway toward the stairs.

Since I'd had to help Emily with her homework, it took

me a while to finish mine. By then the laundry was sounding as silent as a tomb. Hungry for company, I went down the stairs to chat with Papa.

However, I took the precaution of peeking first and saw that he had given up any pretense of reading. He was just sitting in his chair, staring off into space. As I walked through the empty laundry toward the back, the big rooms made me feel even sadder for Papa. By now he and Mama should have been scrubbing up a storm.

Mama was at the kitchen table with a piece of paper in front of her and a stub of one of our old pencils that she had economically kept. The unsharpened end was chewed. As she sat, her fingers idly played with the beads of the abacus.

Though Papa knew mathematics, he approached the accounting the way Bobby approached soap—very tentatively. Papa meant well; but if he got some insight into a poem, he would abandon everything to write down the idea and post the letter to a cousin in Pittsburgh. Though Mama could neither read nor write, she had become the book-keeper out of sheer exasperation. Mama couldn't cipher the formal way we did, but it didn't mean that she was ignorant. She could do sums faster in her head than we could—and with an abacus she was a match for anyone. She knew to the penny how much money we had, keeping most of the figures in her head and occasionally making marks in a ledger book in her own system of notations.

I drifted inside the kitchen. "Mama, why isn't the laundry busy?"

"The people walk by as if we're invisible." Mama clacked the beads around vigorously. "Or they just point and laugh." I could tell she was just as worried as Papa. "How was school?"

I wanted to tell Mama about my star-fisher day, but I also didn't want to add to her troubles. "It was all right."

"And the lettuce sandwiches?" she asked.

I shook my head. "No one found out."

71

Mama glanced down the hallway. "Where are Bobby and Emily?"

"They went to some friends' houses for supper. Papa said it was okay."

Disappointed, Mama turned back to her figures. "Why didn't you go, too?"

"Maybe I wanted to be with you."

Mama hunched her shoulders even more. "Thank you for gracing us with your presence."

I always seemed to be reaching out my hand and getting it slapped. And those were the times when I sometimes looked at Mama and saw a stranger—not just someone who was unknown to me, but a real stranger. I saw her with American eyes: saw the little woman with the funny skin and the odd eyes.

And suddenly I knew how the star fisher's daughter must have felt: belonging to both the earth and the sky, she must have seen everything through a double pair of eyes. And I wondered if she felt just as angry and mixed-up inside as I did. I was mad at myself for seeing her that way—at the same time I was still mad at her for being so mean.

I didn't say any more because that would have been playing into her hands by providing her with another occasion to deliver another lecture about how wild and disrespectful I was. Being alone was better than being with Mama when she was in one of her moods, so I quickly exited into the courtyard that separated our laundry from the rear of Miss Lucy's big house.

Flat stones led to her kitchen as well as ours, but the rest was dirt. In front of her house was the small vegetable patch. Miss Lucy was in the middle of her patch on her knees.

"Oh, hello. How was school?" When she pulled at some weeds, they came away in her hand with a ripping sound.

Odd, but I found myself wishing that I could tell the truth to Miss Lucy even though she was a stranger. Maybe I'd had to do too much fibbing that day. Maybe I'd had enough of trying to be strong and not getting appreciation for trying to be.

"Fine," I said in a small voice.

Miss Lucy studied me for a moment. *"Would you like some tea?"*

I couldn't help laughing. *"Do I have a cookie face?"*

"The worst kind. You've got an ice cream face," she teased, going along with the joke. *"But I didn't make any."*

"I could use a cookie," I said, helping her to her feet. Hunger overcame my feelings of being disloyal to Mama. Lettuce sandwiches and crackers do not fill you up for long.

But when we went inside her house, Miss Lucy wouldn't let me sit down in her kitchen. *"We're just passing through,"* she said as she paused beside the sink. I helped work the pump so she could clean up.

Then, as she vigorously filled her kettle from the pump, I set up a tray with plates, napkins, cups, and saucers. She was silent while she was making tea, for which I was grateful. Then, when the pot was ready, she set it on the tray and, taking off her apron, led me down the hallway to her museumlike parlor.

"There," she said as she set the tray down on a table. *"We'll have tea as if you're proper company. Fetch that chair, Joan."*

In some ways, I missed her sunny kitchen; but I felt too honored to complain. Besides, I had done enough complaining that day. So I dragged a big horsehair chair over as she had instructed.

It was a massive thing, with heavy wooden arms and legs that were carved in the shapes of flowers. A white lacy antimacassar had been hung over the back of the chair.

Miss Lucy sat down in its twin. *"Careful. There's nothing slipperier than horsehair. Once, when I was your age, I was at a party. I did so want to impress the others."*

73

I nodded my head because I could certainly understand that desire.

Encouraged, Miss Lucy began to laugh at herself. *"But I slid right off and landed on my fundamentals."* She leaned forward and whispered as if even now she didn't want anyone else to overhear, *"And everyone could see my petticoats."*

"No," I said.

"Oh, yes," she assured me and poured the tea. *"Six spoonfuls of sugar?"*

I smiled, remembering the other day. *"Just one."*

She smiled back. The spoon clinked merrily on the rim of the cup as she put in the spoonful of sugar. *"Milk?"*

"Just a dab," I said. I was determined to learn.

When she had poured herself a cup of tea, she offered me the plate of cookies. Since Emily wasn't here, I took a half dozen.

"I'm glad to see that you brought your appetite today," she said and helped herself to six also. I suppose the gardening helped work off the cookies because she was a slender little thing. *"Now, where was I? Oh, yes, the chair. I so wanted to make a good impression. And the boy I most wanted to impress just pointed at me. 'Don't they have chairs in Iowa?'"*

I could certainly understand that desire to make a good impression, but I couldn't answer until I had swallowed my mouthful of cookies and washed it down with hot tea. *"I thought you came from here."*

"Yes, but my parents moved to Iowa when I was eleven." Miss Lucy nibbled at a cookie.

"Then why did you come back?" I wondered.

"I had my reasons," she said, and I saw that she didn't want to talk about that anymore. *"But in any event, I was just about your age when I returned."*

And I saw that she understood what it was like to be shy and have to make friends all over again. *"But didn't some of the others remember you?"*

She shook her head, then sipped some tea as she balanced the cookie plate on her lap. *"It just about broke my heart, too."*

"Emily hated to leave Ohio," I informed her.

"She'll get to like it here." Miss Lucy brushed some crumbs from the front of her dress.

"She's already settling in," I said carefully.

"Then she has a knack that I don't have." Miss Lucy began eating another cookie. *"I came back here expecting my friends to remember me, and they treated me like a stranger. And that made me doubly mad because I fought for this town."*

Miss Lucy hardly seemed like the warrior type. *"Fought?"*

She smiled shyly. *"It was just at the start of the Civil War."*

Though there were parades every year commemorating the veterans, it still seemed as remote as Julius Caesar to me. But Miss Lucy had a dreamy expression as if she could still see those days. *"These counties had seceded from Virginia to become West Virginia, and the Confederates invaded. Robert E. Lee and Stonewall Jackson themselves — though this was just at the start of their careers."*

"Did you kill anyone?" I asked.

She seemed surprised that I would even think so. *"Of course not. The Union troops were having trouble communicating with one another. A commander would send out a soldier with a message and the Confederates would bushwhack him. But then the commander here got the idea of sending me. He figured that the Confederates wouldn't suspect a ten-year-old girl."*

I wasn't sure whether to believe her incredible story or not; but on the other hand, I didn't want to openly doubt her. *"Couldn't you have been hung as a spy? I mean, you weren't in uniform."*

Miss Lucy gave a firm nod of her head. *"That risk was*

75

explained to me. But I wanted to do my part to end that pernicious trade."

It took me a moment to understand that she meant slavery. *"You were very brave."*

"That's what the commander said." She hesitated and then, as if she had come to some decision, took her plate of cookies and set it down on the tray along with her cup and saucer. *"Come with me, Joan."*

Setting my things back down on the tray, I rose with her. She'd taken her napkin from her lap but still held it in her hand. Curious, I followed Miss Lucy over to the reading stand where the old Bible sat.

When I was standing beside her, she opened the Bible to the ribbon itself and took it out, laying it across both her palms. *"The commander couldn't give me a medal, but he gave me this."*

I examined the ribbon, which had begun to fade with the years so that there were lighter streaks. *"It looks like an ordinary ribbon."*

"Well, yes." She laughed uncomfortably. *"He was in a hurry to march off, so there wasn't time to get anything fancier. So he gave me a keepsake that his wife had given him."* She turned it over, and on the other side I could see someone had written in black ink with a fine, curlicue hand: *"Remember Me."*

I still wasn't sure if I believed the story, though it seemed that Miss Lucy had gone to elaborate lengths to prove a lie — and I just didn't think she was that type. Reverently I touched the ribbon, but then my eye happened to glance at the now open Bible.

The top of the page said *"Genealogy"* and underneath was a list of names with dates of birth and death. *"Are those your family?"* I asked.

"Yes." Miss Lucy placed the ribbon carefully back between the pages and then turned the page to the next set of

charts. _"These are all my family going back to my grandfather. He was one of the first doctors in this area."_

But what I noticed was that there was a date of death recorded with monotonous regularity. I turned the page, which was half-full. Everyone there, too, was dead. Only the box by Miss Lucy's name was open.

"Don't you have anyone else?" I asked.

"They're all here," she said, tapping her forehead.

"I mean living relations."

She took great pains to close the Bible gently. _"I have some distant kin."_

From her tone, I knew that they were so distant as to be effectively nonexistent. I wanted to tell her that we would be her kin, but that didn't seem proper. Suddenly I didn't feel nearly so lonely anymore. At least I had my parents and Emily and Bobby. And perhaps that had been her ultimate intention, after all.

"I'm sorry," I said, clasping her hands.

"Don't be," she said, giving my fingers an answering squeeze.

Eight

*T*hat conversation with Miss Lucy had made me appreciate having my family—as imperfect as it was. After all, we were all that each of us had. So I went looking for Mama, wanting to make up for how our last conversation had ended.

In the kitchen, the rice was simmering on the stove, but Mama wasn't in sight, so I went looking for her. I found her ironing.

"Mama," I said; but she didn't say anything. She didn't even look at me, as if she was still brooding, and I felt my courage melting away. Preparing to sneak out of the room, I started to turn when Mama said, "You think I'm mean, don't you?"

I swallowed. "I never said that, Mama."

Mama sighed. "We have so little money that we can't afford to make mistakes."

"That will change, Mama," I tried to assure her.

Mama looked at me over her shoulder. "My mama was twice as hard on me as I am on you. She said I was no good in the kitchen, so she always had me doing other chores. I told myself that when I have girls, I'm going to be nicer to them. And I try and I try. But we live in America, so you compare me to those lazy American parents. And compared to them, I'm mean."

Other than making excuses about her cooking, Mama hardly mentioned her family. "We try hard, too, Mama. We do more chores than the American children."

Mama tested the tail of the shirt and then straightened out the collar. "I'd like to be the nice one like your father. I'd like you and Emily to have pretty things. But there's never any money. Someone has to be practical."

In her own way, Mama was trying to apologize for her earlier harshness; but I didn't know quite what to say. I realized that we were more used to arguing than to agreeing. "Someday we'll have enough money."

Mama smiled with one corner of her mouth. "That keeps us going, at any rate." Suddenly she began to sniff the air and set the iron down.

Instinctively we raced toward the kitchen. Smoke was rising once again from under the lid.

Mama grabbed a rag as a pot holder and took the pot. When she set it down in the sink, there must have been some drops still on the enamel because they hissed loudly. "What next?" she asked in exasperation.

Mama had left the rag wrapped around the handle, so I used it to lift the lid. The rice was tiny lumps of charcoal.

Papa came into the kitchen a moment later. "I thought I smelled smoke, so I checked and found this in the drying room." He held up one of his shirts with a brown scorch mark in the shape of an iron. In her alarm, Mama had set the iron down on the shirt.

Mama glanced at the shirt and then faced the pot in

the sink. "I won't cry," she kept muttering. "I won't cry."

Papa was enough of a veteran of Mama's cooking to understand when he saw us gathered about the rice pot as if in mourning. "Oh," he said and lowered the shirt.

Despite her earlier words, the tears came anyway to Mama's eyes. Mama was the tough one in the family. I couldn't ever remember her crying—no matter how bad things were—so it was a shock now. And suddenly I realized that she was like a wall that might scrape you if you rubbed against it the wrong way, but that protected you against storm, flood, twisters, and other catastrophes. In my own way, I'd come to depend on Mama no matter how much she scolded me.

More confused than usual, Papa stood there with a philosophy book in one hand and his free hand hovering over Mama's shoulder, uncertain whether to pat her on the back or not.

Suddenly someone began to rap loudly on the back door. Opening it, I saw Miss Lucy with a tray covered by a napkin. *"Good evening. You'd do me a favor by helping me with these leftovers."*

Mama pushed the tray back toward Miss Lucy because our landlady's gestures had made her intention plain. "Tell her no thank you. We're not beggars, and we don't take charity."

Miss Lucy looked at me to translate for her. Once I did, she shrugged. *"But it's just going to go to waste. In fact, I'll have to throw it out soon."*

Mama, though, was firm. "Tell her no. Everything is fine," she assured her through me.

Miss Lucy, however, remained in the doorway. *"Everything is not fine, or there wouldn't be fires."*

It was almost as if Mama blamed me rather than Miss Lucy. "This is my house, and I'll cook the way I want." And she nudged me to hurry up and tell Miss Lucy.

Miss Lucy jabbed her finger at the floor. *"You only rent*

this property. I own it, and I don't want a fire every night."

Mama managed to get the gist of Miss Lucy's words without my interpreting for her. Unfortunately, she was so irritated that she couldn't wait for an intermediary. As a result, she tried to get her point across by sheer force of will. "We've paid our rent. Right now this place is ours, so tell that busybody to leave." She pointed at the same spot on the floor where Miss Lucy was.

Miss Lucy and Mama were both stubborn women. I took Mama's arm before she got us evicted. "Mama, she's only trying to help."

"Then she shouldn't try to come in and boss me around," Mama huffed. However, when I started to open my mouth, Mama poked me again. "Tell her to mind her own business." Again, I was trying to obey when Mama nudged me once more. "What are you waiting for?"

That was just too much. I was growing tired of having to read Mama's mind, and I was tired of having to play the adult when it came to dealing with Americans. "Give me a chance," I snapped.

Mama's nostrils widened as she took a sharp breath. "Don't talk back to your mother."

Sometimes it felt as if I was wrong no matter what I did. Miss Lucy argued with Mama both through me and through pantomime, but Mama's patience grew increasingly thinner. "Tell that busybody to mind her own business," she instructed me. "And use those exact words."

"My mother says no thank you," I said.

Mama, though, had been watching Miss Lucy's face; and when she didn't take any insult, Mama looked at me in helpless fury as if I were being deliberately willful. "What did you say?"

"You don't understand, Mama," I tried to explain.

However, all Mama could see was my defiance. "You tell her what I said—word for word."

"Mama, listen to—"

"Tell her!" Mama barked.

Since Mama wouldn't let me explain, I could think of only one way of sparing Miss Lucy's feelings and saving Mama from making a mistake she would regret. Without another word, I pivoted and started to stalk down the hallway.

I heard Mama's quick steps as she caught up with me and pulled me into the drying room. "Don't you leave me. Come back here."

Everything, though, was catching up with me. "I'm not a dog."

"No," Mama snapped. "A dog would obey."

"Mama," I accused. "You treat me like . . . like I'm supposed to read your mind. Like I'm supposed to be your shadow."

Mama stared at me as if I were some awful monster that had just popped up out of the floor. "You think you're so smart because you can talk English. But you're stupid."

"Mama," Papa scolded gently from the hallway.

The incident in Mr. Edgar's store still smoldered in my mind. "You want me to be real close to you except when there's something shameful. Then you'd rather humiliate me than you."

"That's not true."

"You made me go to the store instead of going yourself because you knew what would happen. That awful Mr. Edgar made me feel like a beggar. It should have been you, Mama. Not me. Mothers are supposed to protect their children."

Mama's hand shot up angrily. "How dare you!"

I felt mean and ugly and getting meaner and uglier by the moment. "I try and I try, but you never notice. It's only when I don't do what you want. And then I'm stupid and lazy. Mama, the umbilical cord got cut years ago."

"No, Mama!" Papa cried.

There was a loud smack when Mama slapped me. At first I didn't feel anything. In fact, my cheek felt numb. But the sound seemed to ring in my ears. Mama had spanked me before, but this was the first time she had ever really tried to hurt me.

I forced myself to sound calm despite the fury I felt inside. "What are you going to do when slapping me doesn't work? Will you try a stick? And if that doesn't work, will you use a shovel?"

Mama stared at me with the funniest look on her face. It was like that of someone teetering on the edge of a cliff, about to go over. "Why did you make me do that? Why? Why?" She brought her sleeve up and wiped at her eyes, and I realized that she was crying.

However, I refused to cry. Blinking back the tears, I ran out of the drying room. Papa tried to catch me, but I evaded his arm and raced through the laundry and out the front door.

Nine

*T*he hurt inside was worse than the pain in my cheek, which was quickly gone. This pain inside wouldn't go away. It kept eating and gnawing inside like some creature trying to break free.

As I stood in a daze out on the street, I heard fingers trickling slowly over the piano keys as someone painstakingly made their way through the musical scale. I glanced at Miss Lucy's house. The lights were already on, so I knew she must have some musical student. And then I noticed the misspelled words newly scrawled on the fence in charcoal.

My first impulse was to attack the fence and tear it down. More and more, it seemed as if Papa had brought us into a trap. Looking up at the sky, I raised my arms and wished I could fly up to the moon. Or just away. Anyplace.

And then I thought of Bernice. Not knowing where else to go in that strange town, I asked for directions to the address I remembered. Though the woman gave me a funny look, she told me how to get there, adding that I shouldn't go there after sunset.

Curious, I started to go the way I had been told. In just a few blocks, the houses began growing smaller and shabbier, the paint flaking when the house had any paint at all. Large warehouses and factories began to appear like squat monsters staring down at the little houses. I stopped at the railroad crossing and looked across at houses that were even more ramshackle. As the sun began to set, a chill breeze began to blow, sending up bits of paper like flocks of anxious birds. In the growing gloom, the windows of the houses began to glow like strange, hard-edged eyes.

A door slammed somewhere and there was harsh, loud laughter. I stood in the weed-grown street among the broken boards of a newly smashed box. It looked like the kind of neighborhood Mister Snuff would live in. My stomach began to twist into uneasy knots. I hesitated, looking across the shining steel tracks. There wasn't a train in sight, so I began to cross.

Broken glass crunched under my feet. Most of the shacks were slowly collapsing into ruin. Here and there was a patch of grass, but most of it was weeds and junk—from broken dolls to frayed old horse collars.

A woman's voice rose angrily from within the thin walls of one house and a man roared back at her. Something broke with a porcelain tinkling. I stopped next door at a ramshackle picket fence where no two pickets quite matched because they were made from scrap lumber. Nonetheless, someone had attempted to paint it white; but they had run out of paint about two thirds of the way through. As a result, you could still see some of the original letters that had been stenciled onto the wood.

I opened the gate onto a scraggly little garden of vegetables that I suspected would have done better if they could have afforded fertilizer. I suppose Ann and her friends might have seen it as a pathetic attempt to imitate the better houses. But to me it seemed like a brave attempt in the middle of the squalor, and I already began to like Bernice's family without having met them.

I started to wipe my feet on the stones before the door and realized that was only making them dirtier. As I did so, I couldn't help wondering what was the great, terrible secret that set Bernice apart from the others. Even the girls from the other side of the tracks shunned her.

There didn't seem anything awful about her—at least to judge from the house she lived in. As with many of the other houses in the neighborhood, the paint was flaking off, though even in the dim light I could see that it had been painted a bright green color once. Burlap sacks had been sewn into fluted curtains over the windows.

From within, I heard a clear, high tenor voice rise sweetly as if someone had started a gramophone. Timidly I rapped at the flaking wood, but they must not have heard me because of the gramophone. Suddenly a woman began to speak angrily—though I couldn't distinguish the words, the scolding tone was unmistakable. However, the singing only swelled in volume; and I realized that the tenor voice was no recording but was real.

Puzzled, I knocked harder at the door. Instantly the singing and scolding both stopped. A plump woman about Miss Lucy's age opened the door. Even so, her hair was dyed an alarming shade of red and bobbed in the latest fashion, with bangs over her eyes. And she wore a dress that showed off her knees.

Before I could introduce myself, she grabbed my hand with breezy familiarity. *"You must be Joan. Come in. Bernie has told us all about you."*

She pulled me into a parlor that was an interesting hodgepodge of furniture—a heavy horsehair chair, a velvet settee with most of the velvet nap worn off. Crates doubled as end tables and book shelves. Even so, there was a warm feeling to the room.

On the settee lay a girl with red-gold hair who looked about Bobby's age. She was lying with a threadbare blanket drawn up to her neck and a wet facecloth folded over her forehead. *"How do you . . ."* A fist flew up to cover her mouth as she began to cough.

"Jo-Jo hasn't been feeling well, poor dear." The elderly woman hastily snatched up a towel from the floor. *"I'm Bernie's grandmother, Nana Lil."*

"It's . . ." The girl coughed again. *"Josephine."* Apparently she preferred to be as formal as Bernice.

"Putting on airs again."

Over in a horsehair chair a sullen man sat in a pair of shoes spattered with paint and trousers equally dotted. He wore no shirt but had on a red flannel union suit. Nonetheless, he had a bow tie knotted around his neck. He had a face and hair to match his union suit. At first I thought it was sunburn.

"I'm Cousin Johnny," he slurred. He tried to look at me; but when he didn't seem able to focus his eyes, I realized he was probably drunk.

I turned away quickly from him. *"Is Bernice here?"* I asked her grandmother.

Nana Lil draped the towel over the arm of the settee. *"No, she's running an errand."*

Everyone in the room seemed tense, though I could not say why—so I was almost glad that Bernice was not home. *"I'm sorry,"* I said. *"Would you tell her that I called?"*

Nana Lil hurriedly began picking up toys and open books from the floor. *"No, please. Stay awhile. Bernie will be so disappointed if she misses you."*

"She'll be like all the rest," Cousin Johnny complained, *"too good for the likes of us."*

"No, I just . . . unh . . . wanted to ask a question about

the homework." I looked at him over my shoulder and saw him reaching for a glass filled with an amber liquid that sat on a crate near the chair. There was a holy card resting over the top of the glass of some woman with hands folded in prayer and a halo over her head. When he lifted the card, I could smell the whiskey odor.

"People used to pay just to stand and listen to me." His head bobbed slightly.

"Really," I said uncertainly.

However, instead of explaining himself, Johnny lifted his head and began singing in a clear, sweet tenor, all trace of the whiskey gone from his tongue, *"Gone are the days."*

Nana Lil slapped his arm with a rag doll. *"Hush. Jo-Jo needs her rest."*

"People used to pay," he muttered and then lapsed into a sullen silence as he sipped from his glass.

Nana Lil bent over with difficulty as if she were feeling stiff. *"You've come a long way to live in West Virginia."*

"Actually," I explained apologetically, *"it's from Lima, Ohio."*

"Lima, Ohio. I think I was there once." She looked up. *"What brought you here?"*

I tried to stay out of her way. *"We had relatives up in Pittsburgh who had a laundry there. And Papa wanted to start his own. So the way the geography goes, it seemed natural to look south."*

"It's very enterprising of your father. Others might profit from his example." Nana Lil glanced over her shoulder at Johnny in a broad hint; but the man ignored such suggestions—or insults, for that matter. With a sigh, she faced me again. *"I played Pittsburgh once. At the Imperial it was."* She nodded to the wall. *"I was the other half of the Terpsichorean Twins."*

Turning politely on my heel, I looked at the wall, which was covered with clippings and flyers—the kind that would be posted upon telephone poles and walls hawking a show. There was a smudged picture of a young woman with a strong chin and a large bosom.

There had been enough hints if I had been paying any attention, but I had been too naïve. I couldn't have felt more shocked than if they had admitted to being thieves and ax murderers. I had paid my money like anyone else to see the people perform on the stage, but like most people I never expected to mix with them. Theater people were . . . well . . . not very respectable either in China or in America, and suddenly I could understand why the other poor girls shunned Bernice. I also understood what had happened this afternoon. Bernice had thought the others might be laughing at her when I had thought they might be laughing at me.

Apparently unconcerned about the effect her news had on me, Nana Lil straightened with an armload. *"That was me about fifty pounds lighter. We're all in the theater, including Bernie's mother."* With the armload of toys and books still in her arms, she came over and pointed with her chin toward a flyer of a young woman with the same pretty smile as Bernice.

Because of Johnny's accusation, I fought the impulse to fly out of the door. *"Lilian O'Malley,"* I read, *"the Terpsichore of Tap."*

Nana Lil blew a wisp of hair up from her eyes. *"Jo-Jo's got all of us beat, though."*

Josephine poked her fingers at the wet compress, adjusting it. *"I want to be a nurse, Grandmother."*

Nana Lil thrust out a hip indignantly. *"And get stuck in this burg forever, kiddo?"*

"You settled here," Josephine said.

"That's because Herby—that's my third husband and the best of the lot," she explained to me. *"That's because my dear, departed Herby's cousin had the kindness to kick the bucket and leave this place to him."*

"Bernice and I have had our fill of traveling," Josephine said firmly.

Nana Lil opened a closet door cautiously against the avalanche of things piled inside. *"You were made for better things than being stuck in some hick town."*

"Nurses work in big cities," Josephine explained equably.

"For peanuts. You and your sister have got God-given talents. You gotta use them. Instead you want to be a nurse and she wants to be a secretary." With one knee propped against the closet door to keep the pressure from swinging it open, Nana Lil began to gather up more junk.

Johnny's head bobbed. *"No sense of beauty or adventure."* Taking a last swallow of whiskey, he began to sing again; and this time Nana Lil didn't try to stop him, even though Josephine clapped her hands over her ears.

"Be quiet," Josephine began to insist, *"please, please, please."*

Nana Lil calmly crossed the room to a set of crates turned on their sides like shelves. Row after row of small glass and ceramic ashtrays sat there. Selecting the nearest, she sent it whizzing through the air so that it narrowly missed Johnny's head and broke against the wall. With a sulky glance at Nana Lil, he lapsed into a sullen silence.

As Nana Lil began to pick up the pieces, I felt I ought to make conversation in the awkward silence. *"You certainly like to smoke,"* I said to Nana Lil.

"I've got my vices but not that particular one." Nana Lil rose with the pieces cradled in her palms. *"But Bernie's mother always likes to have souvenirs from the places she plays in."* I noticed then that one of the pictures had a little notice on the frame: *"Property of the Hotel Savoy."*

"Likes?" I asked puzzled. *"I thought Bernice's mother was dead."*

Nana Lil straightened the picture. *"She might as well be*

*for all these ungrateful children care. They just up and quit
the act right in Buffalo."*

"We were tired of the road," Josephine insisted wearily
as if it were an old accusation.

Not knowing what to say, I peeked over Nana Lil's shoulder and saw that the ashtrays had come from various hotels
and restaurants across the country. *"How many states have
you been in?"*

"Forty-eight," Nana Lil declared, *"and so has Bernie's
mother. Poor Herby nearly got a hernia moving in her
collection."*

In the distance, I could hear the creak of metal as railroad cars slowly swung around a pair of curving tracks.
Through the burlap, I could see that it was getting even dim-
mer outside. *"Well, I should be going."*

Both Nana Lil and Josephine—through a fit of cough-
ing—made polite noises about my staying for dinner. But I
was firm, afraid of after-dinner entertainment and having had
more than enough of Bernice's strange family. They were
lively and interesting, and yet there was something watchful
about them—as if I were an audience of one to which they
had been playing.

Lights were on in the windows of the shacks in shabby
defiance against the night. Eager to get home, I was starting to
trot along when I heard a familiar voice.

"What are you doing here?" Bernice demanded.

I turned to see her with a large shawl draped over her
shoulders against the evening chill. One hand held the shawl
closed around her neck while the other hand held a net bag
in which I could see a brown bottle and a couple of paper-
wrapped parcels.

"I . . . unh . . . got finished with my chores early," I
explained, *"so I thought I'd pay a visit."*

If she had been formal before, her manner was posi-
tively glacial now. *"Well, you were not invited."* She tried to

brush past me. *"You ought to make a lot of friends when you tell them about what you saw. You all ought to have a lot of laughs."*

Grabbing hold of her net bag, I stopped her. *"I'd be a fine one to talk."*

She stared down at my hand. *"Really?"*

When I let go of the bag, it swung back against her hip. *"After all, the only perfect one is Ann."*

The irony made the corners of her mouth twitch up. *"I daresay."*

I held up a hand. *"Are you the one who wants to be seen with me? After all, Ann says I'm a little dark."*

She smiled with relief. *"Ann is an old stuffed shirt."*

I copied her pose. *"I daresay."*

Even in the twilight, I could see the smile that made her freckles rise, reminding me once more of that flock of birds. And suddenly I couldn't help thinking that if a golden feather fell on her sleeve, it would change to a spot of blood, because she was star-fisher stock if ever anyone was.

"Well," she said, *"welcome to the other side of the tracks. Do your parents know you're here?"*

"No." I folded my arms. *"I just had to get out of the house."*

She leaned her head to the side curiously. *"Oh?"*

"I told you things weren't perfect," I said defensively.

She adjusted her shawl. *"If they knew the sort of people you went to visit, they wouldn't care if we lived in a mansion."*

What she said was true. I thought again of what people said about theater folk and their families, but then they had never met Bernice. *"Those prejudices seem a little silly."*

She glanced over my shoulder in the direction of her shack. *"I am not so sure."*

Seeing that look, I knew that I didn't want to hate my family the way she did hers; and then I thought over what her grandmother had said. *"Do you really want to be a secretary?"*

"I don't really care." Bernice looked again in the direction of the shack. *"I simply want something normal."*

I hesitated, remembering what her Nana Lil had called her. *"Do you prefer Bernie or Bernice?"*

"Bernice," she said firmly. In terms of appearance, diction, and even their names, Josephine and she were more respectable than the respectable folks—as if that might change the town's mind.

I wondered where her mother was at that moment but was afraid to ask. I guessed that Bernice's mother was still wandering around the country and perhaps had dumped her children with their grandmother. I had thought Bernice was a bit prim at first, but now I couldn't really blame her. It was her way of separating herself from her family and the people around her. And for all of her primness, she was far friendlier than Ann and the other girls. When I thought of what Bernice had gone through and that she had still remained sweet and kind, it made my own problems seem petty.

Bernice nodded around her at the growing gloom. *"You really should not be here once it's dark."*

I took her hand and gave it a squeeze. *"See you in school tomorrow, kiddo."*

Bernice winced. *"No slang, please."*

She really was determined to change her life. Well, I supposed if I had been shunned by everyone all my life, I might want that, too. *"All right. Whatever you say."*

The shacks didn't look nearly so shabby in the darkness. I took my time walking home, though, because I knew what Mama would say if she knew about Bernice's theatrical background. It wouldn't matter that Bernice wanted to be more respectable than most respectable folks. Mama would have judged her by her family.

It's funny how there are levels and levels of prejudice in the world. The red-faced man hated us for being Chinese; but he would hate someone like Bernice as well for being the child of theatrical folks—just as Mama would herself.

And so, even though holding back on the truth was wrong, so was Mama. And in a way that made holding back all right at the same time. At the crossing, I took my time to check for runaway trains. Once across, I broke almost into a quick run—I was so eager to get home.

Ten

Papa was squatting in front of the picket fence, scrubbing off the letters and trying hard not to show that he was afraid. He could squat for hours that way; but my legs weren't nearly so strong, so I knelt down beside him. I watched his arms pump vigorously and the rise and fall of his thin, wiry shoulders. He seemed ready to clean the fence for the rest of his life. He glanced at me but didn't ask where I had been, for which I was grateful. Taking the wet rag from him, I finished washing off the last of the obnoxious letters.

"They must have run out of paint," I said.

"Until next payday," Papa grunted patiently.

For all of his bookishness, there was a stubborn strength to Papa. Nothing would ever break him—despite all the troubles we were having.

"I wish I could be like you," I whispered.

His head twisted around. "What?"

I was embarrassed by that admission of weakness. "Nothing."

Papa stared at me the way he always did when his American-born children did something strange—almost as if he couldn't quite understand how we could be his. "Mama's inside."

The dirty water sopped through my fingers and dribbled onto the street. "Is she very mad?"

He took the rag from me. "You know Mama: quick to get mad and quick to get over it." He looked at me levelly. "Just remember: she tries her best."

The lights were dim in the laundry. Bobby and Emily had already been sent upstairs. Dreading what was coming, I began to walk down the hall—though it seemed to stretch on forever.

Mama was going over her accounts again in the kitchen. I hesitated in the doorway, but she heard my step. "Where were you?"

"At a friend's house." I added slyly, "She has the best posture in school."

"So," Mama grunted, pleased, "there's one family in this town who know how to make their children behave. What do they do?"

I had selected my words with care so I wouldn't have to lie to Mama—at least, not exactly. "They work very hard. I think they must have been all around the country already."

"They travel? Peddlers?" Mama asked without looking up.

"They . . . unh . . . have suitcases filled with ashtrays."

"What do they need with all those ashtrays?" Mama asked, puzzled.

I explained to her how hotels had ashtrays with their names on them. As I hoped, Mama made the assumption that

Bernice's family sold ashtrays and souvenirs; and while Mama probably would have preferred people more sedentary, she could accept that.

"Selling ashtrays is such a peculiar way to live. Well, I wish you had told someone. Papa was worried." It was always Papa, never her. Mama would rather have died than admit that she had been anxious, too. She glanced up, and when she didn't see me, she turned to the doorway. "Well, don't stand there staring. Come in."

I stayed where I was, though—out of striking range. "I'm sorry, Mama."

Mama twisted around on the stool. When she saw me hovering in the hallway, she gave me a hurt look. "I'm not going to hit you. Come in."

Even so, I drifted in cautiously. "I didn't mean to make you mad."

She massaged her forehead. "It's not just you. It's . . . everything." She added ruefully, "But I guess sometimes I take it out on you."

I stopped near the kitchen table. "And I guess I do the same sometimes."

Mama ran a hand over my dress, fussing with it and smoothing it. "You've grown so tall. Sometimes I forget how much. Look at you—a regular giant."

Under other circumstances, I might have been insulted; but at the moment, thinking of Bernice's family, I was grateful that Mama was who she was. "Papa says that it's the diet here."

"No, it's the soil in this land. It makes everything grow big," Mama insisted. She shoved back a strand of hair from my face. "Sometimes it scares me, you know?"

Mama was the tough one, so it was a shock to hear her admit that she could be frightened. However, when I tried to speak, there was a huge lump in my throat, and it took me a moment to swallow it. "I'm sorry, Mama." I sniffed.

97

We were not big on hugging in our family, so it surprised me when Mama put an arm around my shoulders. "I know."

Despite everything, I couldn't help smiling. "What would your mama have said?"

Mama smiled. "She wouldn't have said anything. She would have just rapped you across the knuckles for being silly." She sighed and looked up at the moon, which had already begun to climb into the sky. "But then I'm silly, too." Her hand massaged my back in broad circles.

I looked down at Mama. "You were married at about my age, weren't you?"

Her fist gripped my fingertips as they lay over her shoulder, and she gave my hand a shake. "That seems like an eternity ago."

I tried to imagine what it would be like to be married, but all I could think of was how frightened I would be. "Were you very scared, Mama?"

"Petrified," Mama said. "It was all arranged, you know. But then I found out that Papa was one of the gentlest of men. And I was grateful."

I pressed myself against her while I thought some more about having a husband like Papa. "My husband will have to like books."

Mama pressed her lips together. "Then you had better be ready to be the practical one."

I tried to defend Papa. "Papa works hard."

"I never said he was lazy." Mama held on to my hand as she stared at the marks on paper that only she could understand. "Papa was never meant for business. He had studied to pass the government exams, which are really essays on poetry and the classics. And then in 1911 came the revolution, and the republic was set up and the exams were ended."

Mama's message was slowly beginning to sink in. I thought of how frustrating it would be to always have to act

98

as the practical one, and I began to understand her a little better. "It must be exasperating sometimes."

"Only when I let it," Mama admitted. "Sometimes when I look at the laundry our customers leave, I see a certain dress that would look nice on you. There are so many pretty things in the world, but you can't have them."

It must have been some effect of the dim gaslight; but it almost seemed as if there were a soft, golden glow about Mama's shoulders; and I thought that if I half closed my eyes I might see a feather cloak.

And suddenly I realized that there wasn't another Chinese woman for probably a hundred miles or more. All Mama had was me and Emily, and we were half-alien to her. In her own way, Mama must have felt as cut off as the star fisher.

"There's no money," I said. Impulsively I stretched out my arm and put it awkwardly around her shoulders to give her a hug.

She stiffened in surprise, and at first I thought she was going to shove me away. But then she relaxed, her fingers stroking the back of my hand. "Still, you're right. I do take you for granted."

"It's all right, Mama."

"No." She tapped her fingers against my hand. "America is so big and there's so much to learn that we depend on you. Maybe too much. Maybe we get mad at you when we really should get mad at America and how big it is. Or maybe we should get mad at ourselves for being so stupid."

"You're not stupid, Mama. America is a big country, like you said."

Mama straightened and looked at me—really looked at me. And I think for the first time in her life, she realized that she had to tilt her head back to do that. I suppose it sounds silly to say that my mother didn't know I was taller than she was, because she knew it in a superficial way. But I don't think it had ever registered deep down inside. Now, her eyes flicking up and down as she studied me, she seemed to understand that I was not only taller but also older and that I might have different needs than I did as a child.

"So is China," she said finally. "And the Chinese stuff pushes out the American stuff. But I'll try to be more American."

"You've already done harder things, like cross an ocean when you were my age."

Mama glanced up at me. "America's so big that we might all get lost."

I reached over and hugged Mama. "I guess it would scare me, too, if we went back to China."

"We are going back," Mama said. It was an article of faith with her and Papa that we would go back. "When we have enough money, we'll live in China at a level appropriate to your father's status."

Mama was always saying that without going into details. I always pictured a big garden where Papa could sit writing poetry while Mama bossed the servants around.

However, the idea of leaving even West Virginia was awful. And I wondered how her daughter had felt when the star fisher told her they were both going back to the sky—back to that strange world that was their birthright and yet was so mysterious and frightening.

When Mama felt me stiffening against her, she hurriedly assured me, "That's a long way off, though."

I thought again of the star fisher's daughter and the questions she must have asked her mother. "Will it be nice there, Mama?"

She patted me clumsily. "You'll like it. You're just scared because you have to cross that big ocean."

I clung to her now. "Will it be really nice, though? Like flying?"

"What in heaven are you talking about?" Mama asked, puzzled.

"Will it have . . ." I struggled to find the right words for my mother, the practical one who always had to have her feet on the earth. "Will it have something wonderful? Will it have magic?"

Mama began to laugh. "Honestly, the older you get, the less I understand you. Sometimes I think you're worse than your father." Mama hesitated, and then on some wild impulse she hugged me back. Years of washing had given her arms the strength of a lumberjack's. "In the meantime, I promise to try harder to be more American." And then she shoved me away brusquely to hold me at arm's length. "Have you eaten yet?" When I shook my head, she smiled. "Neither have I. Help me get supper."

With both of us working, supper did not turn out as badly as on other nights. But you didn't need a very educated nose to know that something had gone wrong. We were in the middle of salvaging what we could when we heard the knock on the kitchen door.

When Mama opened it, Miss Lucy folded her arms. _"Mrs. Lee, I really must insist on helping you. I simply cannot have more fires."_

Mama could get the gist of what Miss Lucy said from just her expression and tone. Instantly, Mama began to bristle. "That busybody's got some nerve. You tell her—"

If I had learned one thing from my visit to Bernice, it was not to let a lot of silly prejudices blindfold you. It was important to meet with the person and not the notion. So I did what I should have done earlier and put a hand on Mama's arm and interrupted her. "Mama, her family's all dead except her."

That jolted Mama upright—as if she had smacked up against a brick wall. "No one?"

I knew from Papa that we had a chain of cousins, uncles, and aunts extending all the way from China to Pittsburgh and from there to New York as well as San Francisco. It was hard to think that anyone could be as alone as Miss Lucy. "No one.

She's lonely, Mama. She just wants to help."

Mama rubbed her elbow doubtfully as if, despite all the years she had been here in America, she still found it hard to believe. "So she's the last?"

"Yes." I glanced meaningfully toward Miss Lucy's house and then back at Mama. "I saw it in her holy book. They keep a chart of the family."

Mama gazed at Miss Lucy as if Mama had just stepped out the door and found our landlady the victim of some terrible accident. "How . . . horrible."

Mama was standing there stunned, and her reaction puzzled Miss Lucy enough to make her forget her original indignation. Looking back and forth from one to the other, I hunted for the words that might build the bridge between them; but the words were like so many stars that wriggled away like slippery fish.

In the awkward silence, Miss Lucy cleared her throat. *"Is there something wrong?"*

"No," I said; and then, because I thought I ought to explain the conversation between Mama and myself, I fibbed, *"We were just discussing your offer."*

Miss Lucy dropped her arms. *"I realize that every country has its own customs. How would someone offer help to another person if we were both in China?"*

I could put Miss Lucy's words into Chinese, but the concepts were a little harder. However, feeling sorry for our unfortunate landlady, Mama now felt obligated to try. It took a bit of discussion with Mama before we hammered out an answer.

"Every village has a clan," I explained. *"Your family would naturally help."*

Miss Lucy fussed with her sleeve. *"And if you weren't near your family?"*

It took a little more head scratching for Mama and me before I could answer, *"That just couldn't happen."*

Miss Lucy's chin touched her chest as she pondered her

response. Finally she looked up. *"Well, couldn't . . . couldn't you think of me as family?"*

Knowing what I did of American families, I tried to ease the disappointment for Miss Lucy. *"I don't think you know what you're getting into,"* I told her.

"Neither do you," Miss Lucy said. *"I know what it's like to be a stranger. When I moved back here from Iowa, I didn't know anyone. And though I had family here, they were all so much older and set in their ways."*

By this time, Mama was impatient about being left out of the conversation, so she tugged at my sleeve. When I had finished translating, I was surprised that Mama nodded her head in comprehension. "It's true. You can be a stranger in your own family." I think she was thinking back to her own life in China before she had been married. She nudged me. "Especially if you're the youngest and everyone thinks of you as a pest. Make sure you tell her that."

When I had repeated Mama's words in English, it was Miss Lucy's turn to nod her head. *"Exactly."*

Mama and Miss Lucy stared at one another as if, despite the barriers of language and custom, there was now some kind of bond—however tenuous and easy to break.

"It would be nice to have a sister," Mama concluded but added hastily, "But only here, in the kitchen." And she confided to me privately, "There's no American really ready to belong to a Chinese family."

When I had translated everything but the last sentence, Miss Lucy hooked her arm through Mama's. *"We'll be cooking cousins."*

Mama was surprised by the physical contact, but she recovered and patted Miss Lucy's hand in silent concord.

"But, Mama," I said, "Papa said no."

"After two smoky suppers," Mama noted, "he's ready to change his mind."

Eleven

*B*ernice was a little shy the next day, as if waiting to see whether I was going to blab everything to the school; but she warmed up when she realized I was going to keep her secret. That made it awkward again around lunchtime because I still couldn't eat with her.

"It's family stuff," I said and leaned in close to whisper, *"You understand."*

She gave me a sympathetic nod. *"Of course."*

We could still walk home together; but when I got to the laundry, it was the same old story: no customers.

Papa looked even more worried than before. Without any chores to do once my homework was finished, I headed down toward the kitchen; and when I didn't find Mama there, I stood uncertainly, listening to the laundry—but it was silent inside.

Then, from across the courtyard, I heard Miss Lucy say, *"Hello."*

However, before I could answer, I heard Mama speak. *"Hel-lo,"* she said, drawing out the syllables.

"Hello?" I said, puzzled.

"Hello," Miss Lucy said firmly.

"Hello," Mama said with more conviction.

"Very good," Miss Lucy said approvingly.

As I neared Miss Lucy's house, I saw three small pies laid out in a row upon the windowsill, with a neat little triangle missing from each. They smelled like apple pies, but only sort of. Something didn't seem quite right, although I couldn't put my finger on it.

Peeking over the lower door, I saw Mama and Miss Lucy in their aprons with their sleeves rolled up and white flour dusting their arms. Mama compared her pale white arm to Miss Lucy's. *"Like sisters."*

"Like twins," Miss Lucy agreed with a laugh. *"Now let's try this one: good morning."* She pronounced the last two words with elaborate care.

Picking up a rolling pin, Mama began to flatten a lump of dough. *"Goodmor-r-r. . . ."*

Miss Lucy went over to her stove. *"Good morning,"* she said again. I suppose she thought it was more efficient to teach Mama cooking and English at the same time.

When I knocked on the doorframe, Miss Lucy turned around and greeted me as brightly as usual. *"Hello. How was school?"*

"It was all right." Opening the bottom half-door, I stepped into the kitchen.

Mama laid her rolling pin down and got a knife. "Are you hungry?" she asked but didn't wait for an answer. "Have some pie." She went over to her latest creation, which was still so hot that steam rose from it.

There was a clatter as Miss Lucy slid a plate off a stack. *"This smells like the best one so far."*

Cutting off a neat wedge of pie, Mama slid it onto the plate and brought it over to me. "Tell me what you think."

Holding the plate in one hand, I broke off a small piece of the pie. The crust felt as hard as plaster—which wasn't too promising an omen. And when I took a bite, I wished that I hadn't. If this was Mama's best so far, I hated to think what the previous ones had been like.

"Well?" Mama asked expectantly. "Be honest."

Believe me: when people say that, they never mean it. My mind raced desperately from cliché to cliché. I gained time by pointing at my still-masticating jaw—though I didn't know which was worse: to keep on chewing or to swallow. Mama was still hovering by my elbow when I eventually choked down the sample. "It's . . . unh . . . different," I said. I thought I had chosen the right words, but Mama's face fell.

Glancing back at the windowsill, I now understood that each wedge-shaped hole in the pie was a missing biteful. If they had been any good, there would have been more missing. All those tries by Mama and every one of them wasted.

Mama looked in the same direction and realized that I knew. Embarrassed, she wouldn't face me but picked up the rolling pin. "I'll get it right this time."

Under Miss Lucy's coaching and encouragement, Mama's elbows and arms flew in a show of determination. I started to feel guilty for the things I had said yesterday. After all, Mama was only trying to keep her promise to be more American; but I was afraid she was in for a terrible disappointment. However, before I could say anything, a man appeared in the doorway. His head was bald and round, and he was dressed in a black suit and white shirt. *"Good afternoon, Miss Lucy."* He smiled at Mama and then at me. *"Are these your new tenants?"*

"There aren't many secrets in this town, Reverend." Miss Lucy laughed. And then she introduced us to the Reverend Bobson.

106

Mama straightened, self-conscious about the rolling pin in her hand. *"Hello,"* she said with great care.

The Reverend seemed pleased that Mama could speak English. *"Hello. Welcome to our town."* He held out his hand.

Mama stared at it uncertainly until I prompted her. "You're supposed to shake it. It's the American way of greeting."

"Yes, yes, I remember," Mama said nervously. Wiping her hand vigorously on her apron, she took his hand and pumped it up and down.

"Whoa, you've got quite a grip for someone so little." The Reverend massaged his hand once Mama had let go. *"Well, don't get the wrong idea from Miss Lucy. We're not nosy in this town. We just care about one another."*

Miss Lucy rocked up and down on the balls of her feet. *"That's what the cat said before curiosity killed it."*

"And what do you say?" The Reverend beamed at Mama.

Instead of looking to me for a translation, Mama was determined to conduct the conversation on her own. *"Hello,"* she said again.

I forced myself not to smile. After all, Mama was trying her best to let me lead my own life.

The Reverend Bobson knitted his eyebrows together and then gave an uncertain little laugh. *"Yes, well."* He clapped his two big hands together and turned to Miss Lucy again. *"I was going to ask if you could donate a pie to our pie social tomorrow night."* He eyed the pies on the windowsill. *"I see that I came at the right time."*

Miss Lucy waved a hand politely at Mama. *"Actually, they're Mrs. Lee's."*

The Reverend Bobson clasped his hands in front of him. *"You're a baker, too? Then our town is twice blessed."*

Mama's head automatically started to turn toward me. However, remembering last night, she stopped. Licking her lips uncertainly, she tried to hold a conversation on her own. *"Good morning,"* she said.

The Reverend seemed a little startled. *"And a good afternoon to you, too."*

Miss Lucy glanced at me, puzzled, as if she was wondering why I wasn't helping my mother. And when I just held my peace, Miss Lucy tried to explain herself. *"Actually, he was talking about your pies."* She jabbed a finger exaggeratedly at the pies on the windowsill.

Of course, Miss Lucy's explanation was just as incomprehensible, since it was in English. Mama stood in a panic, her fingers twisting and untwisting the hem of her apron.

Suddenly she seemed so fragile that I began to understand why she had insisted I go to Mr. Edgar's instead of her. I suppose Mama faced enough daily humiliations at the laundry counter because of her lack of English—and that couldn't have been easy, considering her pride. On the one hand, she had to appear almost ignorant with strangers.

On the other hand, she also wanted to protect us, like any other normal parent, and instead she had to depend on us to deal with the Americans. That made for a tough balancing act—as if she had her right foot on one galloping horse and her left foot on another. And at that moment, I began to see her for what she was: she was just an ordinary human being—like her daughters—who was trying to do her best. And that made me love her more.

Feeling guilty for my own hard words, I put my hand on Mama's arm and put their statements into Chinese for her.

Mama gave my fingers a grateful squeeze. "Tell him that I'm just a student." She jabbed a floury finger at Miss Lucy. "She's the teacher."

I translated what Mama had said—and then jumped at the chance to get rid of my pie. *"Here."* I held out the plate before Mama or Miss Lucy could stop me.

Miss Lucy's hands flew up in alarm. *"Maybe the next one."*

"No, don't go to any bother." Taking the plate, he picked up the slice and stuffed it into his mouth.

His face had the oddest expression as he began to chew. And his face got odder with each passing moment. He tried to smile as he chewed, breathed noisily through his nose, tried to smile again—like a hen laying her first egg and not at all sure what she had gotten herself into.

All the while, it was silent in the kitchen while Miss Lucy stood anxiously at one of the Reverend's elbows and Mama at the other. Finally, the Reverend Bobson put down the plate and swallowed with elaborate care.

"Have some more," Mama immediately urged.

The Reverend understood Mama's gestures without having me translate her words. Taking out a handkerchief from his pants pocket, he dabbed at his mouth. _"You know, I just had lunch, so it's hard to eat another thing."_

Mama hesitated as she looked at Miss Lucy and then at me—as if she were reluctant to bother me; but it was Miss Lucy who prompted her. _"What is it, Mrs. Lee?"_

Through me, Mama asked what a pie social was.

"A pie social," Miss Lucy supplied, _"is where people bid money on a pie. The highest bid wins. And all the money goes to the church."_

When I translated, the Reverend Bobson watched the whole process with interest. _"Would you care to make a contribution, Mrs. Lee?"_

This time I didn't wait for Mama to look at me before I began interpreting. Mama thought a moment. "Is it the thing to do?" she asked me. When I nodded my head, she mulled that over some more. "I don't want to shame my children anymore."

"Forget Mr. Edgar," I said, wishing I'd kept everything to myself.

"I heard you the first time," Mama said and dipped her head as if she'd come to a decision. "Tell him I'll bring a pie."

I was aghast. "Mama, you can't."

"If Miss Lucy will lend me the ingredients." When I hesitated, Mama nudged me. "Go on."

"I didn't think you wanted to beg," I said, trying to head off trouble.

"You heard her yourself," Mama argued. "She's like a sister. You can borrow anything from family. And anyway, we can pay her back in trade."

It was like riding on a train and seeing that the bridge over the river was washed out. I could see an even worse disaster looming for the family that dwarfed anything that had taken place already. "Mama, he doesn't want a pie. He wants money."

"We don't have any cash to spare," she said to me. "And even if we did, you can't auction money. Tell him." However, when I hesitated, Mama frowned angrily at me. "Tell him."

"Mama," I begged, trying to stall for time, "I don't think you understand—"

"You want us to fit in, don't you?" Mama demanded. "Well, tell him what I said."

I flushed at that reminder, wishing that I could have bitten off my tongue for having said that. "I'm sorry I said anything," I said desperately.

Furious, Mama pointed at the pies on the windowsill. *"Pie,"* she said. *"Pie, pie, pie,"* as if repetition could get her meaning across.

Grabbing Mama's arm, I forced her to lower it. "Mama, don't," I pleaded.

Mama shook me off. "I shame you if I do, and I shame you if I don't." She turned then to Miss Lucy. *"I borrow . . . things."* She pointed at the ingredients on the table. *"Okay?"*

Though Miss Lucy seemed surprised, she waved a hand grandly at her kitchen. *"Of course, you can borrow what you need. And you don't have to worry about paying me back."*

The Reverend Bobson, though, had flinched when he understood Mama's offer. *"A Chinese pie?"* he asked hopefully.

Mama glanced at me as if she didn't trust me to translate for her anymore, but I did. "Tell him it will be an apple pie." She indicated the pies again. "Like those."

However, Mama's gestures had already made her meaning plain. _"How . . . unh . . . interesting,"_ the Reverend observed and left hastily before he could be forced into eating another bite.

For the rest of the afternoon, Mama kept practicing while Miss Lucy and I tried to help; I now felt responsible. Miss Lucy fussed and coached. I worried and fetched whatever Mama needed. And with each new attempt, I would cross my fingers and whisper, "It will be good. It will be good. It will be good."

They were never very good, though. By sunset I knew we were facing a worse situation than the lettuce sandwiches. It was one thing to have the town know how poor we were. It was another thing to have them laugh at us.

I tried to find a diplomatic way of bringing up the subject. "Mama," I said quietly.

She shoved a strand of hair from her eyes, her fingers leaving white strips of flour across her damp forehead. "What?"

Mama's failures sat upon the windowsill, six of them now; but Mama ignored them as she leaned forward, rolling the dough hard and vigorously as if it were all of our troubles she was trying to flatten. I could tell that she was just as worried as Papa, but the actual act of baking was helping to distract her.

I picked up a scrap of dough from the table and fingered it like a lump of clay. "Mama, this might only make things worse."

Mama set the rolling pin to the side. "Things never come easy for you and me." Almost shyly, Mama raised a hand and patted my arm. When she took her hand away, she left the mark of her fingers in flour. "But we're tough."

After she said that, I couldn't tell her that I was afraid she

111

was going to be the laughingstock of the whole town. No matter what I did, I was going to lose. I threw the lump down with a little thumping sound. "You're right, Mama."

Mama turned to the oven and opened the oven door, letting the heat roll into the kitchen as she slid another miniature pie out and held it in her apron. "Now, who's going to try this one?"

Though Mama spoke in Chinese, Miss Lucy understood Mama's questioning look. However, by then she was as tired of sampling pies as Mama and me. All three of us just stared at the pie.

Then Bobby popped into the kitchen with his shirttails hanging out and dirt streaking his face. *"Hello, Miss Lucy,"* he said in English and added in Chinese, "I'm hungry. What's for supper, Mama?" He looked from the pie in Mama's hands to the other little pies. "Are we opening a bakery, too?"

Mama smiled at Bobby. "Try this one," she said. Her face looked perfectly innocent. I hadn't realized how much guile my mother had.

However, Bobby knew Mama's cooking too well to fall for that. "That's all right. I'll have a lettuce sandwich."

Though Mama kept on smiling, her voice developed an edge. "Try it."

Bobby glanced at the pie and then at me. "How were the other pies?"

I didn't dare look at Mama when I spoke. "They're all terrible."

Mama gave up any pretense of maternal affection. "Try this one," she ordered. "And I mean this one." She emphasized the last two words.

Bobby began tucking in his shirttail miserably. "Do I have to?"

"Eat" was all Mama said.

Grateful that it was him and not me, I got a clean fork. "Here, Bobby."

Bobby silently mouthed the words "I'll get you for this." Then he took the fork, but it hovered above the plate.

"Mama—" he started to beg.

"Eat," Mama commanded.

Bobby held the fork poised over the plate, staring down at it.

Mama was merciless. "Eat."

Bobby slipped the fork into the piecrust with excruciating slowness—as if the pie itself might explode at the slightest jar. But as the fork poked into the pie, a sweet smell filled the kitchen.

Encouraged, Bobby lifted a forkful of pie and put it into his mouth. At first he didn't chew. He just left the mouthful there in the front part of his jaw, ready to spit it out.

A moment went by and then another, and still Bobby didn't swallow. Instead, he stood there, breathing noisily through his nose because he couldn't breathe through his mouth.

Putting down the pie, Mama held out a towel to him. "Here."

Bobby spat out the mouthful. "I'm sorry, Mama."

Mama reached behind her neck to try to untie the apron, but her fingers, stiff from all that baking, could not undo the knot. "At least now the pies have the smell right."

Bobby glanced at the failed experiments sitting upon the windowsill. "What are we going to do with all those other pies, though?"

"Nothing goes to waste. They're our supper," Mama said practically and presented her back to me.

"Oh," I said quietly as I helped her untie the knot. I made a mental note to boil a lot of water so we could make enough of Papa's medicinal tea—the kind that was good for indigestion.

Twelve

*T*he next day in school a new thought occurred to me that made me feel even worse: What if Ann belonged to the Reverend Bobson's congregation? Things were bad enough without giving her more ammunition. In the back of my mind, I could already hear her comments about our clumsy attempt to ape American ways.

Sometimes Bobby could get Mama to stop doing things that neither I nor Emily could. So even if I'd had a real lunch, I couldn't have let Bernice sit with us. Unfortunately—ever the optimist—she followed me out to the fence. *"It's family matters still,"* I tried to explain.

At first Bernice looked as if I had hit her in the stomach; but then her old habits came to her rescue, helping her hide her disappointment behind a polite mask. *"If you say so."*

That made me feel awful because while Ann had been

Ann and her friends had been just as stuck up as ever, Bernice had made up for a lot of it. I watched her walk away proudly with an erect posture that Mama would be pleased with. Turning to the fence, I called loudly to Emily and Bobby, who reluctantly broke off their games and came to eat with me.

Quickly I told them of my new fears as I opened my lunch bag. "We're different enough without calling attention to it."

Bobby had spread his open at about the same time. "Oh, no," he groaned.

"What's the matter?" Emily asked; but when she looked into hers, she let out a little moan, too. "Apple pie."

Somehow Mama had snuck parts of last night's experiments into our lunches. Resolutely I took out my sandwich. "Throw it away later," I said.

Both Bobby and Emily chewed at their sandwiches thoughtfully, no doubt worrying about what their newfound friends might say, and occasionally glancing at the sandwich bags with their deadly contents.

"I'm open to suggestions," I said.

Bobby turned his sandwich around and around in his hand as if studying it from all angles. "You know Mama. Once she gets a notion in her head, it's like trying to stop an avalanche."

Emily made a face at her lunch bag. "We could drop her pie on the way to the social."

We considered and scrapped several plans during lunchtime, having to adjourn at the bell without reaching any solution except for Emily's suggestion. As I dumped my piece of pie into a trash can, I just hoped it wouldn't come to that.

Feeling guilty, I made sure after school to locate Bernice so I could walk with her. Outside, a worried Bobby and Emily were waiting for me. When I arched my eyebrows in silent hope, both of them shook their heads.

I let Bernice do most of the talking as we headed for home, my mind only half on what she said. Though she'd had more adventures than most of our classmates, she was reluctant to talk about them. Instead, she wanted to talk about the books and magazines she'd read. She was a ferocious reader. I gather that the local library had a hard time keeping up with her appetite. Bernice studied the middle class like a spy studying the strange customs of a tribe because she was determined to pass herself off as one of them.

As we paused beside our laundry, ready to separate, she caught me by surprise when she asked, *"Would you like to study at the library tonight?"*

Without thinking, I shook my head apologetically. *"I wish I could, but I might have to help my mother get ready for a pie social."*

To my discomfort, Bernice said wistfully, *"Oh? I love pie."*

It was bad enough to be humiliated in front of strangers, let alone my new friend. Even if she was theater people, she was still American. Would the disaster at the pie social make her think I was too foreign?

Seeing me hesitate, the sensitive Bernice misunderstood. *"Perhaps, though, I should not eat so many sweets."*

What could I do? I was trapped. If I didn't invite her, I'd hurt her feelings twice in the same day and perhaps lose her as a friend; but if I did, I was sure I would surely go down in her estimation. With a sad shrug, I said, *"No, of course you should come. It's at the Reverend Bobson's."*

It was Bernice's turn to hesitate. *"I didn't realize it was going to be at a church."*

"I don't think you have to belong to his congregation to go," I explained. *"We don't."* In actual fact, I hoped that was the reason that would prevent Bernice from going.

There were times when Bernice sounded as if she had just read an etiquette book. *"My sister and I shall be looking forward to it,"* she said gravely.

116

My shoes felt as if they were made of lead as I clumped up the steps and into our laundry. There hadn't been any more customers than the other days; but Mama was over at Miss Lucy's, baking up a storm; and we all had to eat at home tonight to help Mama get rid of the leftover pies. There was something wrong with each one: the crust was too hard on some, the spices wrong on another, and so on.

Mama herself looked thoughtful after a long, careful chew. "At least none of these are as bad as my first tries."

Bobby, Emily, and I glanced at one another. Though that was true, the pies were still capable of bringing ridicule from the entire town.

"Maybe you ought to experiment some more," I suggested hopefully.

"My teacher says I'm so close," Mama said, referring to Miss Lucy. "I think this last one may be it." She nodded to a pie that rested on a shelf. "I just wish I could cut into it to make sure. But" — she raised and lowered her shoulders in an elaborate shrug — "sometimes you just have to have faith."

I glanced at Bobby, who jerked his head toward Emily as if suggesting that her solution was the only one. After only a few bites, each of us shoved our plates toward Papa. "Why give them to me?" he asked helplessly.

"Don't waste them," Mama ordered. "Eat." She was already running hot water into the laundry tubs.

It seemed funny that the only things that got washed in the washroom so far were our clothes and us. The hot water only filled a few inches in the great tubs, and we shivered as we took quick sponge baths. Mama had hung sheets up over the windows for privacy. As I got dressed in my best clothes, Emily whispered to me, "You know what you have to do."

I eyed her. "Why me? Why not you or Bobby?"

"Because," she argued, "you're the only one she'd trust."

"So," I complained, "I'll be the only one who can betray that trust."

"You know I'm right," Emily insisted.

When everyone was clean and dressed, we gathered again in the kitchen. After a critical inspection and minute adjustments, Mama finally gave us her approval.

Taking a breath, I turned toward the shelf and started to stretch out my arms. "I'll carry it for you, Mama."

To my dismay, Mama elbowed me out of the way. "And have you take credit for my newest baby?"

As Mama lifted the pie lovingly from the shelf, I turned to the others and spread out my arms helplessly. Cradling the pie tin's rim against her stomach, Mama shooed us out into the rear courtyard where Miss Lucy was already waiting.

The church was a big brick building with a tall steeple and white trim. Its bell could have been heard across the whole valley. The church itself was dark, but there were stairs leading down in the basement; and light spilled from the open door like a warm, golden welcome mat. People were already streaming into the basement, their voices high with excitement; and loud, cheerful laughter boomed off the basement's low ceiling.

It was a large room with tables set up at one end and chairs lining the walls. There was a woman with almost silver-blue hair piled up on her head who sniffed when she saw us enter, but Miss Lucy ushered us right past her to the table where the pies were. Bobby immediately spotted two of his classmates and headed off into a corner with them. Emily met some girls she knew and darted away through the crowd as nimbly as a fish in the sea. I cringed inwardly when my worst fears proved true and I saw Ann with a pie. Havana was there, too, along with Henrietta and Florie, trailing her like two cabooses after the locomotive. However, I didn't see Bernice at all, so perhaps the disaster would not be as complete as it could have been.

I followed Miss Lucy and my parents — feeling like some odd pet that they were towing along. Miss Lucy seemed to know everyone, and she introduced us to each of them. But that only reminded me of my own isolation, so that I felt even uglier and lonelier. By the time the auction started, my head swam with names.

The Reverend Bobson stood behind the center table, tapping a little wooden hammer against the surface. Instantly the crowd grew silent.

"Now," he intoned solemnly, *"we have a pie by our foremost baker."* He pointed his hammer at Miss Lucy. *"I know Old Jim there has been waiting all week for this."* He swung his hammer toward a cheerful man with a walrus mustache.

"You bet," Jim agreed. *"Fifty cents."*

The Reverend waggled his hammer. *"Shame on you, Jim. Trying to steal a pie like this. And in church, too. We're going to keep an eye on that bank of yours."* The Reverend looked around the room. *"Are you folks going to let him get away with that?"*

It was corny, but everyone laughed, including the Reverend. It was a shared joke, and it was for charity. By the time he was finished, the Reverend had driven the price up to three dollars. (Jim got the pie.)

Papa leaned over toward Miss Lucy. *"You should open bake store."*

Miss Lucy tried to be modest. *"It's all for charity."* But no one else seemed surprised at the high price. Apparently, her pies always did well at the socials.

The Reverend Bobson sold several more pies—sometimes teasing, sometimes joking, but always driving the price up and up. Though when he held up Ann's pie, the Reverend didn't have to worry about driving up the price because Jim put up his hand right away. "Five dollars for that magnificent pie!"

"Oh, Daddy," Ann scolded from across the room, "give someone else a chance."

As the whole congregation burst into laughter, Ann's father sheepishly lowered his hand; but the original bid was

119

too steep for anyone else, so he got Ann's pie—and he wound up buying two more pies.

Then the Reverend held up Mama's pie. *"And now we have an apple pie baked by our newest neighbor, Mrs. Lee."* He tapped his hammer. *"Who'll make a bid?"*

No one, not even Mr. Wood, put up a hand or said anything. To our left, I heard someone titter. I thought it sounded like Ann or one of her friends; but when I started to twist around, Mama grabbed my arm and gave me a warning pinch. "Be still."

"Where's your sense of adventure, folks?" The Reverend looked all around the room, but still there were no takers.

As Mama's cheeks began to turn a bright red, the Reverend cajoled his congregation. *"Now, now, is that any way to greet her?"*

Mama turned to Papa, but Papa kept his eyes resolutely ahead of him and his arms at his sides.

Mama leaned in close to Papa. "Bid," she whispered from the side of her mouth.

Papa cocked his head toward Mama. "I'm sick of pies," he whispered back. "I've had pie for breakfast, lunch, and supper."

"Bid," Mama insisted.

Papa dug at his shirt collar. "We can't throw money away like that."

"Bid," Mama ordered.

All this time, the poor Reverend had been trying to get someone to make a bid; but for once his powers of persuasion seemed to have failed him. I glanced around surreptitiously, and I was glad that Bernice wasn't here to see this.

"You're embarrassing the children," Mama hissed.

Papa glanced around him. Emily was clustered with some of her friends by the punch bowl. Bobby was off in a corner, perched with some of his friends upon some crates. Each had their fingers crossed. If Papa bought the pie, we just might avoid a terrible humiliation.

Papa, though, misunderstood what we were wishing for. "They seem fine to me."

"Bid," I begged Papa.

"Bid," Mama said and then added ominously, "or else."

I glanced curiously at Mama, but I never did find out what that "or else" meant. Papa's hand shot up. *"Ten cents."*

The Reverend Bobson instantly pounced on the bid. *"I bet Mrs Lee knows something. Who'll make it twenty-five cents?"*

Miss Lucy started to put up her hand, but Mama stopped her and shook her head. Having Papa bid was one thing— that wasn't charity—allowing her new friend to bid was another.

"Twenty-five? Twenty-five?" the Reverend asked hopefully. But when no one else put up a hand, the Reverend did a very kind thing—considering his own experience of Mama's pies. Putting down his hammer, he dug into his own pocket and counted his change. *"Well, I'll take my own advice. I'll put up twenty-five cents out of my own pocket."*

I started to slump in my chair, but Mama hissed, "Sit up straight."

Picking up his gavel again, the Reverend tried to coax some more bids and seemed disappointed when his own ploy was unsuccessful. Rapping the table, he solemnly intoned, *"Sold."* Setting Mama's pie aside, he went on to the next one.

When the auctioning was all done, people came up to pay for their pies. Taking Emily's hand, a girl who must have been her friend, Janey, pulled her toward Mr. Wood; and over in the corner, Bobby was following his friends forward to join the clumps of children hovering near Mr. Wood as he stood in line. As it turned out, his four pies weren't for him. After he had paid for them, he shared the pies with the children around him. They clamored for Miss Lucy's first; and after that, I kept hoping that Ann's pie would make people sick; but all of Mr. Wood's selections were wolfed down.

Soon Bobby's mouth was smeared with streaks of blue and purple—though he must have been sick of pie by now, he'd had nothing for supper. I saw Ann there, too, with a face just as messy as Bobby's. However, so far no one had tried Mama's pie.

Mama gave me a worried glance and nudged me. "Go on," she urged and pointed toward the mob of children around Mr. Wood.

I looked around, grateful that as yet Bernice had not shown up. I might just escape with only a partial embarrassment if we could leave soon. "No, thank you. Can we go home now?"

Mama, however, misunderstood and gave me one of her patented nudges. "You have to keep trying to make friends."

I stayed right where I was, ignoring the digging elbow as I had learned to do. "I will. It's just that I've had enough excitement for one night. Can we leave?"

Concerned, Papa put a hand to my forehead. "Now, Mama, maybe she ate something that didn't agree with her."

He'd forgotten, though, what we'd been eating all that day. Mama fairly bristled. "Are you suggesting that there was something wrong with my pies?"

Just then Bernice and Josephine stepped into the doorway, both of them dressed in their Sunday best. Holding hands, they entered the basement, looking around. They saw us just about when the Reverend Bobson did. I cringed as they all began to converge on us at the same time.

"We've been here long enough, don't you think?" I asked Papa desperately.

Mama, however, folded her arms, as immovable as a mountain until someone tried her pie. "We just got here."

The Reverend Bobson reached us first, presenting the pie to Papa with both hands. *"Mr. Lee, my conscience wouldn't let me rest unless I let you have your wife's pie."*

Before I could breathe a sigh of relief, Bernice and her sister joined us, smiling a silent hello. I tried to smile back at

122

them bravely. Inside, I was praying that we could take the pie and escape home.

Unfortunately, Miss Lucy took a teacher's pride in her pupil and was just as determined as Mama to have the pie eaten in public. *"You ought to try a piece first, Reverend,"* she suggested.

The Reverend tried to pat his stomach with his free hand. *"Well, I've had so much pie to eat that . . ."*

Miss Lucy wasn't about to let him off the hook that easily. *"It's really one of Mrs. Lee's best."*

"All the more reason not to deprive Mr. Lee," the Reverend said meekly.

Miss Lucy folded her hands in front of her in her best schoolteacherish fashion. *"No,"* she said firmly, *"you bought it. You should have at least one piece. Waste not, want not."*

The Reverend held up a hand anxiously. *"Really, no, I couldn't."*

Though Miss Lucy looked at him reproachfully, the Reverend ignored her. But just when I thought we were going to emerge from the social with some dignity, Bernice cleared her throat politely. *"May I have a slice?"* she asked in a small voice.

Everyone turned around at about the same time to stare at her and her sister, and the Reverend Bobson blinked as he tried to place them.

I thought I understood why she had asked and tried to warn her off. *"Don't feel obligated."*

Bernice gave me a small, puzzled look but persisted according to her notion of good manners. *"But I am famished."*

At that moment, the woman with silver-blue hair bustled over. *"Of all the nerve,"* she said. *"Get out."* I stared at her in shock, thinking that she meant us; but she bulled right past me and waved her hands at Bernice and her sister. *"You don't belong with respectable folk."*

The Reverend Bobson put his hand on the woman's

shoulder. *"If not here, where else, Mabel?"* I guess he had finally recognized the two sisters after all. *"Didn't the Lord himself say, 'Suffer the little children to come unto me'?"*

"With some children, it's more suffering than anything else," Mabel huffed, but she beat a hasty retreat to a corner where she could glare safely at all of us.

"Forgive Mabel," Miss Lucy said in a loud, theatrical whisper. *"She hasn't been the same since she took the train trip to Florida. Her body came back, but they lost her brain along with her luggage."*

"Miss Lucy." The Reverend Bobson tried to frown in disapproval — without much success.

"I'd like a piece if I may," Bernice repeated.

Mama and Papa had been smiling through the whole exchange without understanding, but Miss Lucy turned to Papa now. *"Do you have a penknife, Mr. Lee?"* And she pantomimed cutting into a pie.

Though Papa didn't understand the words, he was used to being swept along by events because he was already digging out his knife and handing it to her.

I put my hand on Papa's arm to stop him. "Papa," I said urgently, "this has gone far enough." And then I turned to Mama. "The whole town thinks we're funny enough as it is."

"So? Let them think what they like," Mama insisted. "We know the truth."

Aware of all the others watching me without comprehension, I argued, "I'm sorry that I ever asked you to be more American, all right? Now let's go."

Mama looked up at me challengingly. "You're a Lee. You're never going to be like the others. You can't let their laughter rule your life." And from the way she studied me, I felt just like a frayed skirt that Mama was trying to decide whether to throw out or to save.

And I found myself wondering, What if the star fisher's daughter had wanted to be like the others? She would never have flown. Impulsively I reached down and took the knife from Papa and handed it to Miss Lucy.

She took it with a polite nod and snapped out the blade. *"Let's make sure you get a nice big piece."*

Anxiously I watched Miss Lucy cut a slice of pie and put it on Bernice's open palm. Half of me realized just how terrible it was to be ashamed of Mama, but the other half — a shriller half — regretted letting Miss Lucy cut the pie.

Bernice stared around the little circle and then looked down at her dress. *"Why is everyone staring? Is there a stain on me?"*

I tried to shake my head in warning to Bernice, but Mama caught me. *"Eat,"* Mama insisted.

I held my breath, waiting for Bernice to spit it out; but when she kept on nibbling unconcernedly at her pie, Mama patted her free arm. *"Good girl, good girl,"* she murmured gratefully. And, of course, Josephine had to have a slice, too, so that Mama beamed a grateful smile at both of them. "And," Mama observed benevolently, "what good posture they both have."

With a glance at the pair who were eating in blissful ignorance, the Reverend gave a little cough. *"You know, Miss Lucy, maybe I'll try a slice after all."*

When Miss Lucy had given him one, he nodded to Mama and took a bite, chewed, paused, chewed some more; and then without saying anything more he wolfed down the rest of the piece.

"Well," he said, shaking the crumbs from his hand, *"that was the best quarter I ever spent."* He called to a passing man with sideburns like copper wire, *"Harve, try some of this. It's almost as good as Miss Lucy's."*

Miss Lucy cut the pie into slices; and when Harve tried a bite, he nodded his head approvingly. *"Not bad, Mrs. Lee. Not bad at all."*

As Harve ambled off, munching happily at his slice, Miss

125

Lucy explained. *"Harve's the town barber and better at getting the news out than any newspaper."*

The Reverend waited for me to finish interpreting for my parents before he wagged his index finger at Mama. *"You're quite a joker, Mrs. Lee. What did I eat yesterday? One of your daughter's experiments?"*

As soon as I had translated for Mama, I waited to put her reply into English; but to my surprise her lips moved as she practiced her English words silently before she replied.

Guiltily I said to her, "I'm sorry for what I said, Mama. Let me help."

However, Mama held up a hand; and then with all the intensity of a tightrope walker on a slippery rope, she plunged ahead into the conversation all on her own. *"No, mine."* Mama hooked her arm through Miss Lucy's. *"Good cook. Good teacher, too."* She glanced at me as if to say, You see, I'll do it on my own. And inside, I silently applauded her courage. It was like trying to walk through a woods with only the sketchiest of maps.

A bearded man with a derby in one hand came over at that moment. His eyes darted around the room as if there wasn't much he was missing. When his glance fell on Bernice, I saw her cringe a little and begin to turn as if she wanted to sneak away; but I caught her hand and held it tight, and Bernice gave me a nervous smile.

The man in the derby seemed to make a mental note to himself about what I had done, and then he turned to the Reverend. *"Harve says to try some of the pie."*

The Reverend Bobson pretended to hold the pie over his head. *"Too late, Eustace. You had your chance. Anyway, you don't belong to this church. What are you doing here?"*

Eustace beat his derby against his leg. *"Reverend, a politician belongs to every church. And a sheriff especially has to be impartial."*

The Reverend sniffed. *"I don't notice you upstairs praying, just down in the basement eating."*

"*If you held your church services on other nights besides Sundays, like you do your pie socials, I'd be there.*" Eustace was a good head taller than the Reverend, so it was easy for him to snag a piece of pie from the tin plate. "*It's all right,*" he declared after he bit into it.

"*And he ought to know: the sheriff's sampled free meals all over town,*" the Reverend teased and winked.

And before long, the Reverend Bobson had run out of pie to share and people were still coming over to see if there was any left.

And though she couldn't understand their words, their smiles made their meaning plain enough. Though she was pleased, Mama did not believe in showing emotions in public. Instead, she folded her hands decorously in front of her. And though she didn't smile, I knew she was feeling immensely satisfied. "You see?" she asked me. "It pays to be stubborn."

Thirteen

The next morning, Emily and Bobby could bask in the reflected glow of Mama's triumph because their friends all wanted to know when she was going to bake again. As we walked up Main Street, Havana fell into step beside me. *"I don't think we've been properly introduced."* She smiled nervously at me.

I didn't think she had forgotten the introductions on my first day in school. However, I played along with her to see where she might be going. *"No, I don't think we have. I'm Joan Lee."*

To my surprise, she balanced both books and bag lunch to put out her hand. *"Havana Garret. My daddy runs the hardware store."*

"Yes, I've seen it," I replied politely.

We walked along in awkward silence, our heels clumping along on the street. A Chinese might have taken another half hour making polite conversation before she got to the point, but I knew I could always outwait an American. _"Look,"_ Havana said, _"I got to have a bite of your mama's pie, and I've been wondering all night where she learned to bake."_ She added, remembering her manners, _" 'Scuse me for asking."_

This was the longest conversation I'd had with a classmate besides Bernice. _"I don't mind if you don't mind my asking you a question."_

"Shoot," Havana said.

I frowned, trying to phrase the question carefully. _"How did you get your name? Did your family visit Cuba?"_

"Nope. I was named after my daddy's favorite type of cigar. He's told that story to the whole town." Havana seemed resigned to the fact. _" 'Spect he'll tell you soon enough — 'specially if your mama keeps on baking for the church like that."_

I couldn't think of anything else to say but _"Your father has quite a sense of humor."_

Havana smiled with only one side of her mouth. _"The funniest."_

I glanced around and then inclined my head toward her. _"Do you ever . . . unh . . . wish you could . . . unh . . . change your name?"_

Havana grinned. _"There was a time when the name was a burden, but I've gotten used to it, and now it's always a good icebreaker with strangers."_

"I bet it is." I kept my part of the bargain by telling her about Mama's lessons, and then waited for her to excuse herself. Instead Havana went on chatting with me all the way up the hill to the high school.

Then, once we were in the hallway, I was also "properly" introduced to Florie and Henrietta.

Having all this attention was a heady feeling after the last few days. It was funny, but it was as if all the words had been penned up inside me — only I hadn't been willing to admit it and now they all came rushing out; and even in that brief time, it crossed my mind to be grateful in general to whoever first thought of putting apples into a pie and in particular to Mama for being so stubborn.

At that moment, Ann and her clique sashayed down the hallway. If I thought she'd be friendly, too, though, that hope quickly died. She just stood there with a smirk on her face as she stared at us hard. It would have taken a miracle to change Ann. It was such a shame, too, because her father seemed so nice.

Under her gaze, I broke off in mid-sentence, waiting for the others to leave; but Havana made a point of putting her hand on my wrist and leaving it there. *"What were you saying, Joan?"*

Ann murmured something to her group and there were superior snickers as they swept by. I should have known that a church would count for much more in a small town than the local class queen. The sense of relief washed away my previous thoughts. *"I . . . um . . . forgot."*

Henrietta hugged her books together against her stomach. *"That Ann is so stuck up. I can't tell you how much she's teased me about my name."*

"Or me," Havana said.

Bernice drifted into view, studying us as if we were strange birds that had suddenly plopped down in the school hallway. I caught her eye and nodded for her to come over, but she just kept on moving along, looking sad and forlorn.

For a second, I didn't know what to do. Part of me knew she was doing the generous thing by avoiding me, and yet part of me couldn't abandon my first friend in the town. I'm ashamed to say that I almost let her slip away; but she and I were kin in some odd sort of way, so I called out more loudly, *"Bernice."*

This time she stopped, but she still wouldn't come

toward me. The others had fallen silent—from shock, I think. Feeling just like an express train that was thundering toward a bridge that was out, I managed to juggle my books so I could wave her over.

As Bernice slowly made her way through the crowded hall, I waited for Havana and the others to whirl around and turn their backs on both of us; but they just stood there.

Once Bernice was standing in front of us, I felt as if I could only blunder along. *"Bernice, do you know every-one?"* And then I just held my breath, praying that they would remember that their minister had not kicked Bernice out.

It was, perhaps, a test of loyalty to their church, but after several long heartbeats Havana nodded at Bernice. *"No, I don't think I do."*

After introductions, we chatted for just a little bit more until the warning bell sounded and we split up to go to our classes. As Bernice and I rushed toward English class, I said, *"I want to thank you for last night. Without you, I don't think anyone else would have tried my mother's pie."*

Bernice swung her head to stare at me in puzzlement. *"I was curious."*

"There are a lot of things I'm curious about but I don't think I'll ever try."

"Without curiosity, you wind up being dead in the head." Bernice rapped a knuckle against her forehead for emphasis.

I couldn't help giggling. *"Like Ann."*

Bernice couldn't help laughing. *"I guess we both have curiosity bumps as big as our heads."*

I stopped, studying her solemnly. There were plenty more differences than similarities between us, but maybe that curiosity bump was a stronger bond than all the rest. *"Friends?"*

Bernice shuffled her armload of books so she could hold out her right hand. *"Friends."*

I had to do the same juggling act to free up a hand to take hers. Gravely we shook hands and then, almost embarrassed, we hurried after the others.

The strange thing was that the wonderful dream did not end when school finished. While Emily and Bobby each had their group of friends to walk with, I had my own. Havana, Henrietta, Florie, Bernice, and I walked toward Main Street together; and in no time, Havana, Henrietta, Florie, and I were joking as if we had known each other for years. Bernice, though, was a bit more withdrawn. I suppose after years of being so hurt, I would be, too. However, she smiled at the right times and seemed to have stopped being uncomfortable. At any rate, I felt that I had done the right thing sticking by her.

When we reached Main Street, Bobby, Emily, and I parted from our friends—it was nice to be able to use that word—and went through the gate. I knew something was different as soon as I opened the door. I could feel the warm steam blowing into my face and could smell a hot iron on starched cloth. And then I saw Mama behind the counter handing half a ticket to Ann's father, Jim.

"Monday, Mis-tah Wood," Mama was saying.

With a nod, Jim Wood stowed his half ticket into his pocket, turned, smiled at us, and walked out the door.

I went behind the counter and helped pin the other half of the ticket to the shirt on top of the bundle. When Papa filled out the ticket, he used Chinese characters; but when Mama did, she drew little pictures that only she could interpret. "We've had customers?"

"Enough," Mama said. She was a fervent believer in never boasting. "I've got chores for you all, but first . . . " Mama said to me and pressed some money into my hand. She must have dipped into the savings in our cashbox. "You go to the store and get a chicken for tonight."

"And maybe Monday I can get some *baloney* for some real sandwiches?" I asked hopefully.

132

Mama counted out the precious coins and piled them one after another on top of the counter. "We haven't had that many customers yet."

"Mama, you'll never change."

When I tried to hug her, she held me off. "I should hope not. I've had enough change to last me a lifetime."

"Oh, Mama." I hugged her anyway, and she suffered patiently through it.

"Go on. Don't waste time on that nonsense." She began bustling around the counter. "You've got chores to do when you get back." And she gave me a look that told me I had better scoot, so I did.

As proud as a duchess, I walked into the Emporium; and when I asked for a nice juicy chicken, I deliberately clinked the coins in my hand. And after that it was _"Yes, miss,"_ and _"Please, miss,"_ from Mr. Edgar.

I was savoring the sensation as I approached our laundry, reliving my small shopping spree, so I didn't notice Mr. Snuff until he jeered at me. _"Hey, chinky-chinky."_

Mr. Snuff and his lean friend were back, lounging against the church. Clutching the precious bundle against my stomach, I made a point of ignoring them and turning into the laundry. I was going to be strong and patient like Papa. I saw that they had painted new slogans on the fence. Though I didn't give them the satisfaction of lowering my head to actually look at it, I noticed that their spelling hadn't improved any.

Inside the laundry, Bobby and Emily were already working without any pestering from me. Papa was in the drying room when I found him after shopping. Lines crossed the room at even intervals, and the shirts and sheets and all kinds of things hung from the lines, water pattering down on the floor like a regular rainstorm.

When I told Papa what I'd seen, he went on calmly pinning up a shirt sleeve. "Get me some water." He picked up an old rag.

My eyes grew wide. "But they're still out there, Papa."

Papa held his head up proudly. "And I am a businessman. I have a right to be here, too."

I got the bucket for Papa, and all of us followed him into the front of the laundry. "Stay here," he cautioned and went outside.

The two men jeered drunkenly when they saw Papa. As we watched from the windows, Papa went to work as if they were no more than a couple of crows cawing at him.

However, Miss Lucy heard them as well because she came walking out of the alley between our laundry and her house. In her hand, she had a garden stake, as if she had yanked up the first thing at hand. As soon as they saw her, the two fell silent, shifting uncomfortably as they leaned against the church.

It wasn't long before an old black Ford came chugging up the street with the derbied sheriff at the wheel. When he stopped deliberately at the laundry, Mister Snuff called across the street, *"Evenin', Eustace."*

The sheriff looked as if he didn't relish being so familiar with the pair. *"Evening,"* he said as he climbed down from the car. *"Is this what you called me about, Miss Lucy?"*

"It is."

Papa stopped and slid over to the side hopefully to let Eustace study the men's handiwork.

"Well?" Miss Lucy inquired. Her toe had begun tapping impatiently.

"Let's go inside where we can talk," the sheriff said quietly.

As soon as the three of them were inside the laundry, Miss Lucy turned to the sheriff. *"Eustace, are you or are you not going to arrest them for defacing my property?"*

The sheriff took off his derby and studied the crown. *"Did you see them do it, Miss Lucy?"*

"No, but—"

The sheriff picked some lint from the crown of his

derby. *"Did anyone here see them do it?"* He looked up and glanced at each of us. *"Then you don't have a very good case."*

Miss Lucy pointed her garden stake toward the street. *"Ask them. Just ask them. They're proud as peacocks."*

The sheriff fiddled with his derby's hatband. *"Well, I could arrest 'em. And maybe you could even get a jury to convict 'em. Then what?"*

Miss Lucy blinked. *"Well, they'll go to jail, of course."*

"They'll go to jail," the sheriff agreed and paused for a moment, *"but their friends won't."*

"Then you'd better start building a bigger jail," Miss Lucy said.

"Miss Lucy, right now the boys are happy just with being a nuisance." The sheriff beat his thigh with the derby. *"But you up the stakes on them, and they just might ante in."* He took us in one by one. *"I'd hate to see the second-best baker in the town get hurt."*

All this time, I had been translating softly for Mama and Papa. Mama put her arms around Emily and looked at Papa when I translated the last sentence. Papa sighed. "Tell Miss Lucy it's all right."

When I had spoken for Papa, Miss Lucy got an even more stubborn look. *"But it's not all right. Eustace, you're just afraid of not getting reelected."*

The sheriff studied a brass button on his vest that needed to be sewed on tighter. *"The thought has crossed my mind,"* he allowed unashamedly. *"I like my job and I'm good at it — most of the time."*

Miss Lucy drew herself up in indignation. *"I'll call the police then. You're the county, but they're local."*

"You could," Sheriff Eustace observed laconically, *"but they'd tell you the same thing."*

"They're crossing the street," Bobby said and repeated himself in English even as Mama jerked him away from the window in alarm.

135

Miss Lucy took a deep breath through her nose. *"Eustace?"*

Sheriff Eustace stood there unhappily. *"They aren't going to do any real harm while I'm here."*

"This is not to be borne," Miss Lucy snapped and stormed out of the laundry before anyone could stop her.

"Sheriff," I begged, *"you have to stop her."*

To my astonishment, the sheriff simply took out a set of cigarette papers and a bag of tobacco. *"Ever go fishing, young lady?"*

I wrinkled my forehead in puzzlement because I didn't see what fishing had to do with the pending fight. *"No."*

"Once you bait the hook, it's up to the fish to catch itself." Setting his derby back on his head, he began to roll a cigarette for himself with well-practiced motions of his fingers.

Outside, Miss Lucy angrily jabbed the garden stake at the fence. *"Did you do this?"*

Mister Snuff spread out his arms in an elaborate show of innocence. *"Do you see any paint?"*

Both Mister Snuff and his friend easily outweighed Miss Lucy, but that little bird of a woman stalked right toward them as if they were no more than two stray dogs.

"Where did you hide the paint?" she demanded. *"I know you have it around here someplace."*

I think Miss Lucy surprised both of them. Mister Snuff spread his legs and clenched his fists defiantly, but the other man tried to sidle in back of his wider friend.

Miss Lucy had to crane her neck back to talk to Mr. Snuff face to face. *"You were always a sneak, Sidney Skags."* And then she looked around Sidney at the other man. *"And you, Hank Barlow. Don't you try to hide behind Sidney. It didn't work when you were in my school, and it won't work now."*

Hank stepped away from behind Sidney. As tall as he was, he hung his head like a small boy who had been caught red-handed. *"Now, Miss Lucy —"* he started to say.

"Picking on poor newcomers." Miss Lucy planted a fist

on her hip as she stared at the embarrassed Hank. *"Aren't you ashamed?"*

Sidney, though, didn't scare as easily as Hank. *"Why are you protecting these heathen?"*

"Sidney, you were a bully when you were a boy, and you're a bully now. And there's only one way to deal with bullies." Miss Lucy's hand suddenly darted toward Sidney's head, and she seized his ear between her thumb and fore-finger.

"Ow, ow, ow!" Sidney's head jerked toward Miss Lucy when she yanked his ear down. *"Let go!"* He raised a hand to knock her arm away, but Miss Lucy had quick reflexes for someone her age. Or perhaps it was from years of practice. At any rate, she rapped the garden stake smartly across his knuckles. *"Ow!"* He wrung his hand painfully in the air.

"If I can't knock some sense in at one end, I'll try the other." Miss Lucy brought the garden stake down with a loud whack on Sidney's behind.

Sidney scrunched his eyes shut painfully as he cried out, *"OW!"*

Hank gave a nervous little jump — as if he knew all about Miss Lucy's arm and what she could do to a guilty person.

His head still tilted toward her, Sidney glared at her. *"I'd kill a man for doing what you just did."*

Miss Lucy let go of Sidney and stepped back. *"Don't let my skirts stop you. Just go right ahead and try."*

Sidney used his good hand to rub the sore spot. *"Don't you push me."*

Hank pulled desperately at Sidney's shoulder. *"You can't fight an old lady."*

"Who's old?" Miss Lucy demanded.

Sidney shook off Hank's hand. *"I should've settled the old hag's hash a long time ago."*

Miss Lucy smiled confidently as if — man or boy — she could read Sidney Skags like a book. *"But before you do, I'll let everyone know about the time — "*

Sidney reared up as if Miss Lucy had bit him in the ankle. *"Shut up,"* he growled, grabbing her by the arms.

Miss Lucy looked up at him defiantly. *"That's the difference between you and me, Sidney. I can go before my Maker with a clear conscience."*

"You old bag of bones," Sidney roared and threw Miss Lucy down so that she hit the fence and plopped down on the pavement.

Sheriff Eustace was out the door the next moment. *"That's enough, Sid. Or I'll have to take you in."*

In his anger, it took Sidney a moment to realize what the sheriff was saying. *"You wouldn't."*

"Assault and battery on Miss Lucy?" Setting the rolled-up cigarette between his lips, he helped her to her feet.

"But she hit me first." Sidney looked over his shoulder at Hank for confirmation but didn't wait for his friend to nod.

"As far as I'm concerned, it's our word against yours." Sheriff Eustace produced a match from his coat pocket.

"She's a chink lover," he complained. *"It'd never stick."*

"Well now, that's an interesting proposition, isn't it?" The sheriff struck the match on the fence. *"Her family's done a lot of good. Half the town is buried in the land the Bradshaws donated for a cemetery — and the other half is headed there. Besides, she's taught a chunk of the town, and most of us think kindly of her — she never had to hit us."*

"The boys won't let you get away with it," Sidney blustered.

"Maybe." Sheriff Eustace bent his head slightly as he lit his cigarette. *"And maybe not."*

They eyeballed one another for a moment, and then Sidney's shoulders sagged like a balloon running out of hot air. *"It ain't gonna end here."*

Miss Lucy was brushing herself off. *"If I find one more thing on my fence besides whitewash, I'm filing a complaint."*

"It ain't gonna end," Sidney swore, but he let Hank pull him away.

Sheriff Eustace helped brush Miss Lucy's elbow. _"That should hold them for a while."_

"For the wrong reasons," Miss Lucy grumbled.

"Take what you can get, Miss Lucy," the sheriff advised.

"And what happens when Sidney begins to forget about today?" Miss Lucy demanded. _"His memory was always woeful—he never made it past the five-times table."_

The sheriff puffed nervously at his cigarette. _"Now, that's up to you and the rest of the good-thinking people, I figure."_

Miss Lucy considered that and then suddenly squinted up at the sheriff. _"I didn't know people in your church were allowed to smoke."_

"We're not," the sheriff said and threw his cigarette down. _"At least in public."_

Miss Lucy scratched the side of her head as if she was remembering. When she lowered her hand, there were dirt stains on her cheek. _"And I did so spank you—when you were seven."_

Sheriff Eustace grinned sheepishly. _"I was hoping you'd forgotten."_

Miss Lucy stretched up an arm and gave his ear a playful tug. _"But I won't ever tell."_

The sheriff ground out the cigarette under his heel. _"At least in an election year."_

As soon as Miss Lucy had stepped into the laundry, Mama stopped her and, like a good sister, used a sleeve to wipe Miss Lucy's dirty cheek. _"Thank you,"_ Mama said. I had been translating for Mama and Papa all during the exchange with Sidney and Hank—though it had been a little hard to fill in the gaps for Sheriff Eustace's laconic remarks.

Miss Lucy suffered the cleaning like some small kitten with its mother. _"There's nothing to thank me for. If I'd been a better teacher, Sidney would have learned some manners."_

When I had translated, Papa nodded his thanks to Miss Lucy. "But she mustn't do it again. We will deal with them."

Outside, the sheriff's car coughed grindingly into life as

I put Papa's words into English. *"And whose turn will it be next? Retired piano teachers? Besides, they just made it my fight, too. They shoved a Bradshaw."* She patted Mama's arm to make her stop her ministrations.

I was explaining to her even as she was exiting through the front door. I broke off to turn to Mama and Papa. "What's she going to do?"

It was always first things first with Mama. "She's going to have dinner just like us," Mama said. Putting her hand to my back, she propelled me toward the kitchen.

Fourteen

That Saturday morning, Mama had lowered one of the ironing boards that Papa had mounted on a wall and begun to iron one of Mr. Wood's shirts. Papa and I were at a small table near her, folding up some of the clothes and wrapping them up in blue paper.

When the bell that hung over the door tinkled, Papa grunted, "I'll get it." Papa had the transaction down to a routine which required only his few words of English.

As Papa stepped through the curtain, I heard the Reverend Bobson greet him brightly. *"Good morning."*

"Morning," Papa said. Buttons clicked on the counter as Papa sorted through the Reverend Bobson's bundle. *"You pick up Monday."*

"Make it Tuesday," the Reverend Bobson teased. *"I wouldn't want you working on Sunday."*

When the bell tinkled again, the Reverend said, *"Morning, Harve."*

"Morning, Reverend. Morning." The latter greeting must have been for Papa.

"Morning." Papa.

When the bell tinkled a third time, there was another round of greetings, as if the new customer was also from the Reverend Bobson's church. A moment later the bell sounded again, and Papa thrust his head through the curtain. "I need help."

Once I joined Papa at the counter that morning, I never got to leave, because there was a steady stream of customers, including Sheriff Eustace. He seemed especially fascinated by the ticket, which Papa had written out in Chinese. *"Say, what's this mean?"* he asked, pointing to a phrase.

"Dress shirt," I translated.

The other customers who were waiting craned their necks to peek at the sheriff's ticket. *"Really?"* the sheriff asked.

I pointed with my pencil. *"In Chinese, it literally means 'big sweat coat.' "* I pointed to another phrase. " *'Little sweat coat' means it's an ordinary shirt."*

Holding the ticket between the fingertips of both hands, the sheriff studied it from various distances. *"Why?"*

I shrugged as I took it back from him. *"Because that's what they looked like to the first laundrymen."* I made a note on it to repair the button on the vest the sheriff was also leaving.

As Papa cleared the counter for the next pile, he looked at me. "You see," he declared. "There really was a town full of dirty clothes for us." He was very pleased with himself.

We had to take our dinner in shifts because there was so much work now. To get some fresh air, I went outside into the little courtyard; and I was still there when Miss Lucy came out with a bucket of whitewash. *"Good afternoon, Joan."*

I jumped to my feet. *"If you're going to paint the fence, we'll do that."*

A smile played on Miss Lucy's lips. *"I think you're all too busy to do any painting."*

I leaned my head to one side. *"I think you had something to do with that."*

Miss Lucy spoke with quiet satisfaction. *"I just made a few phone calls and suggested to some old students that they might want to show Sidney that he doesn't speak for all of us. Their pride did the rest, but thank the good Lord for party lines."*

"Thank you." Impulsively, I ran to her and pecked at her cheek. Miss Lucy was much better at receiving affection than Mama.

"Maybe it will make Sidney and his friends think twice about any more mischief," Miss Lucy said and walked into the alley toward the front of the laundry.

When I finished my dinner, I went looking for Mama and found her in the drying room, where Bobby was feeding wood into the stove to keep the room nice and hot. Emily was standing on a stool, helping Mama to hang up clothes. "Mama," I said, "it looks like we'll have money next week."

"Yes, you can have baloney," Mama grunted.

When Emily started to cheer, I hushed her. "That's nice, but could we do something for Miss Lucy?"

Mama knitted her forehead in puzzlement, but she must have chalked it up to another one of our American whims. "She can have a baloney sandwich, too."

"I mean we have to do something to thank her. Maybe we can take her out on a picnic."

"I'll make the invitation," Emily offered excitedly.

Mama eyed all the clothes doubtfully. "We'll be so busy, though." Mama's pessimism forced her to add, "Maybe."

I almost told her about the telephone calls; but I wasn't sure if she would interpret it as an act of charity—and perhaps be offended—so instead I kept silent. However, I must not have done a very good job of hiding the struggle because Mama studied me intently.

"Is this something one of your American mamas would do?" she inquired.

"Not exactly," I said slowly.

"Is it something that Miss Lucy expects?"

"No." I hesitated. "But you did say you were like sisters."

"Sisters don't always do kind things," Mama observed.

"That's right," Emily chimed in.

"But we do owe her something, so go ahead," Mama said. "Though I can't see how wandering around among weeds and bugs is a way of thanking someone."

Emily dutifully made the invitation for a picnic next Sunday, and Bobby delivered it with all due solemnity across the courtyard to Miss Lucy. On Tuesday we received our first mail at the laundry—an acceptance by Miss Lucy, who asked that we have the picnic between her morning and evening church services.

Emily offered to shop for the picnic, but I was afraid of having nothing except candy, so I went along with her. At the appointed time, Miss Lucy came over to our laundry and we headed down Main Street.

There was a newly painted sign in an appliance store—a sign as big as the window. It showed a lot of bucktoothed, pigtailed caricatures of Chinese in caps and pajamas throwing irons at one another.

In the very center of the sign was the cause of the quarrel—a brand-new washing machine, complete with a hand wringer. The caption underneath declared: *"All the Chinamen want one. Buy one and you'll never want to go to a laundry."*

Apparently Mister Snuff had friends, just as he had claimed.

Even without being able to understand the English caption, Mama understood the picture. She stopped Miss Lucy as our friend was about to head into the store to give the owner a piece of her mind.

"Tell her I'll do it," Mama instructed me.

I looked at Mama, puzzled; but as I turned to speak to Miss Lucy, Mama scooted into the store. There was a short argument punctuated by a series of _wrong, wrong, wrong_'s from Mama spoken in a loud but eloquent voice.

When Mama reappeared, she preened herself. "I don't think I accomplished much, but at least I feel much better."

Though she hadn't understood what Mama had said, Miss Lucy took Mama's arm with a laugh. _"We'd better get you away from here before they call the police."_

Feeling more somber, we followed Miss Lucy up a street which quickly turned into a path that was barely more than a track winding back and forth up the face of a hill. Weeds and flowers grew lushly on either side, and vines wound around the trunks of the tall trees and dripped down from the branches like long strings of green raindrops. And the air was thick and heady with the smell of growing things. It would always be the smell of spring for me. And suddenly I was determined to put away Ann and Mr. Snuff and the appliance store owner for the afternoon. I think we all were.

A bird suddenly called from one of the trees, and Emily turned to Miss Lucy. _"What's that?"_

Miss Lucy had a smaller basket on her arm and a small straw hat pinned to her hair. She paused and studied the green world around us. _"A mocker, I think."_

"That's you," Bobby said and tagged Emily before he crashed up the path through the underbrush. Emily, with more determination than speed, followed her giggling brother.

As Mama watched them go, she bit her lip. From the context, she had understood some of the exchange between Miss Lucy and Emily. "They'll learn all about American birds and not about Chinese ones," she fretted. "What'll they do when they go home?"

145

Papa had been jotting down notes for a poem on one of the old laundry tickets. Putting his pencil away in his suit pocket, he smiled quizzically at Mama. "You've never talked about any Chinese birds except the ones you can cook. I never knew they were important to you."

Mama planted her feet firmly and made another one of her solemn pronouncements. "You should start the Chinese lessons again. I don't want them forgetting who they are."

Papa picked up the heavily laden picnic basket again. Papa, remembering the disastrous attempts up in Ohio, was just as reluctant as I was. "They know already," he said amiably.

I had a blanket and other things over one arm, but I used my free arm to hook through Mama's. "I'm your daughter."

"Humph," Mama snorted. "Big stork like you?"

Papa began to stroll along the path after Miss Lucy. "Better food, Mama. More sleep. You wouldn't go home now."

Mama would never be a democrat at heart. "Not until we're rich and I can have servants—servants who'll carry me wherever I want to go." Still linked arm in arm, she began to walk up the hill with me. But we hadn't taken more than three steps before she jerked me back. "Don't walk with such a big stride," she warned. "You look like a boy."

Papa looked over his shoulder at me. "Mama wouldn't be Mama unless she could fret over something."

I tickled her forearm with my fingers. "Mama, the day's too sunny to worry."

Mama nodded toward some fluffy white clouds to the north moving slowly over the valley. "It could rain, you know." But then she caught herself and laughed. "Yes, well, all right. I'll pretend I'm a rich lady in China and leave all my worrying to my servants."

I tugged her along the path. Feeling ashamed for how I had acted over the pies, I promised, "We may talk and dress and act like Americans, but in our hearts we'll always be Chinese."

"You will if I have anything to say about it," Mama said firmly.

Miss Lucy stopped by a grassy spot surrounding a small, bushy-headed tree with what looked like ripening cherries. They looked like little round pink beads decorating a green gown.

I turned with my back to the breeze so it would help me as I shook out the blanket. Gently, the huge old blanket descended on the grass. There were crisp hisses as I got on my knees and spread it smooth.

Down the hill, I could see the valley—it felt like our valley now. Trees spilled down one side of the valley, across the floor, and up the other side, so that I seemed to be looking down upon the swells of a vast green sea.

From this height, the houses were lost among the leaves. Only the roofs peeked out of the treetops, floating like rafts upon the waves of green. And all over the valley, the sunlight reflected off the hidden windows. Everywhere I looked, the lights winked and twinkled within that green sea.

Just like stars.

And I remembered the star fishers and how they had shone as they had gathered the stars. And I wondered what it would be like to glide back and forth in the sky, shining like a comet.

Suddenly the town didn't scare me anymore because it was like a sea that was all mine to explore. "So maybe I'll fish for a few stars," I said softly.

Emily was already opening the picnic basket. "What?" she asked.

"I think I'm going to like it here," I said and went back to straightening the blanket.

Acknowledgments

I can't say enough for the kindness of Sister Rosemary Winklejohann, who actually called up the Harrison County branch of the West Virginia Historical Society. As I said in the preface, without her, my trip to Clarksburg would not have happened.

I also wish to express my gratitude to Madge McDaniel of that society, who sent on Alice Jo Hess's account of the Davisson family. Then, too, a word of thanks is also due Ian Harris of the Bridgeport Cemetery for kindly showing a stranger around and for looking up old records. Nor should I forget the long-suffering librarians of the Sutro and University of California, Berkeley, libraries for trying to answer the questions I could no longer ask my grandmother, my uncle, and my aunts.

The reference to washboards being a Chinese invention comes from Hommel, *China at Work* (New York: John Day, 1937; MIT Press, 1969); and the story of the star fishers comes principally from de Groot's *Religious Systems of China* (Leyden: E. J. Brill, 1892–1910).